Also by Glenville Obrian Lovell

GLENVILLE OBRIAN LOVELL

GOING HOME IN CHAINS

Glenville Obrian Lovell grew up in Barbados surrounded by sugarcane, shadows and word-magicians. With storytelling all around him—in kitchens, under flamboyant trees at night, in rum shops—he developed a passion for stories which unfolded with the mystery of dreams. He is the author of four novels, several short stories and a number of prize-winning plays, including *The Debating Society* and *Lovers*, both of which were performed at Carifesta. He is a former dancer and one of the founders and the creative director of SAYGE Theater Productions in Barbados. He currently lives in New York. Visit his website or follow him on Facebook or Twitter.

www.glenvillelovell.com
glenvillelovell@aol.com
Follow at:
www.facebook.com/glenvillelovell
www.twitter.com/glenvillelovell

A Chattel House Book

All Rights Reserved

Copyright © 2012 by Glenville Lovell

Cover Artwork: Stanley Greaves

The following stories were previously published: "Court Jesters" as "Coco's Palace" in *Conjunctions* in 1996; "Tall Like You" as "When Blood Runs to Water" in *Shades of Black*, Berkley Publishing Group 2004

ISBN 978-0-9848033-0-9

DEDICATION

For Courtney Quong Lovell: you are that fount of laughter, light and love, from which I will always want to drink. For my brothers and sisters who share many of the same memories and for all the people in Parish Land, Christ Church, who taught me the importance of storytelling. For Essie who understands that stories inspire us to run with the wolves. For the living spirits of my mother and grandmother who gave me my first stories.

GOING HOME IN CHAINS

For Miles

GLENVILLE OBRIAN LOVELL

From my Bajan spirit to you

Enjoy.

CHATTEL HOUSE BOOKS

New York

ACKNOWLEDGEMENTS

My sincere thanks to artist Stanley Greaves for graciously allowing me to use his painting for cover art. I am grateful to Mimi for her honesty and generous words of wisdom. To Chetwyn, Lise, Simone, Kathryn, Janell, Alicia, Merville, Deborah, Elisa, Lenora, Janice, Carol, Ianthe and all of my other Facebook friends who read parts of this collection, as well as my erotic stories: I thank you for your feedback and encouragement. I continue to be inspired by your hunger for good stories, and I love you all for generously sharing the bounty of your curious minds.

going home in chains

SWEET DESTINE

the new uniform spread out on the bed seemed alive somehow, as if it still held his body from the day before. The way the teal epauletted shirt and the shiny navy blue pants played against the seashell sheets made him think of the beach at Paradise Bay and green waves on a hot day. A broad back-home smile crinkled Sweets' dark face.

Sun-cured skin pulled tight against a bony frame made him appear much younger than fifty-five. This smile, unlike the hapless one he dragged through the American Airlines terminal at JFK that cold night back in January, was one of sweet resolve. His after-lovemaking smile reserved for Destine, his wife. It was summer. He was in New York. At last. And he was working.

The thing he remembered most about the night he arrived in New York was the cold. More fearsome than death itself. That cold was a pregnant centipede creeping up his back as he stood under the gloomy airport lights searching the night for his wife. He panicked. Suddenly, as the clangor of New York City mugged his senses, he wished he'd never left Barbados.

To panic was so unlike him. After all, he'd faced death, the greatest of all challenges, and never panicked. Looked it so determinedly in the eyes that Death turned and ran. Not once, but three times.

There was that time his friend, Fowl-Foot, accidentally stuck a knife in Sweets' chest attempting to stop the neighbor's shite-eater from escaping with half a chicken from his kitchen. The five-inch blade Fowl-Foot hurled at the fleeing dog missed and ricocheted off a stone in the backyard right into Sweets' left lung as he sat drinking white rum and falernum. A few years later Sweets fell off a moving lorry transporting canes to the factory. After two weeks in a coma he opened his eyes and whispered the name Destine, a name that signified life and love to him. And who in Sergeants Village, where he grew up and lived all of his life, could forget the day he tried to kill himself 3 years after Destine moved to New York. After all the bragging he did about Destine sending for him once she got settled, about how he couldn't wait to leave the boiling sun and the cane-piece behind for air-conditioned Cadillacs and Dacron suits, how could he now tell his friends that his wife got pregnant by a teacher at her night school and was moving in with him?

Destine rushed back to Barbados with her baby when she got the news that Sweets had drank a whole bottle of the weed killer Gramaxone, which may've worked had Sweets' stomach not been fertilized by Mount Gay's eighty proof white rum. Like everyone else, Destine thought he would be dead by the time she got there, and was returning to make sure that none of his family got their grubby hands on the tiny plot of land where they'd built a modest home together.

But Sweets cheated Death again.

"You ain't make fuh die, boy," Fowl-Foot told him, months later. "A cat got nine lives. But you? You does shite a new life every day."

He begged Destine to stay. She would only promise to stay until he got better. He tried to seduce her with tears, with sweet-talk, with his famous sweet bread, with promises that he'd be a good father to her daughter, Faye.

He tried to stir the ashes of their marriage, attempting to draw her back into the web of their simple life together before she discovered New York and education, and teachers who doubled as lovers. Desperation stoked in him a frenzied passion of such enormity, he felt real fear for the first time in his life.

"Remember the times when I would pretend to be your horse and you would ride my back, ah? Remember that? Remember when I used to walk to Oistins to get fresh sea-eggs for you, ah? Remember that? Remember the times when I used to rub your back and your stomach with camphor oil when the cramps come, ah? Remember that?"

But nothing worked. Destine remembered and forgot in the same quiet breath. Her mind proved harder to change than that of the manager at Buckley plantation where he'd been trying for three years to get a raise. By the time she was ready to leave the island her already plump frame had profited by five pounds from the sweet bread he made fresh every day, but her intent remained fixed. She was going back to the States.

Twenty years later, he arrived in New York to live with that same wife.

So how could one cold night make a man like him panic? Yes, this night was more cavernous, wider and deeper than any he'd ever experienced; and even with all the lights, darker than the despair he felt when Destine told him about her new lover. Yes, the solemn faces in the arrivals hall, the fixed unreflective stares passed around as precisely as a ball on a football field, startled him. This was something he never noticed in the American movies he lived on while fantasizing about life in New York with Destine. He was afraid. He was afraid that even with all his preparation Destine might still reject him as not being American enough.

He must've watched every black movie made in the seventies. At least three times. It all started when Destine came home expecting to bury him. He remembered the way she looked. The way she acted. So American. He was impressed. Talking fast. Laughing loud. Drinking. Smoking. Muthafuckering. Her Bajan accent smothered under an afro-wig fluffier and bigger than Ma Brown's fowl's nest. She was Cleopatra Jones rolled into Foxy Brown. But he was not good enough to be her Shaft, it seemed.

That was why she left him, he believed. He wasn't American enough. Determined to win her back, he made it his business to watch every Black-American movie shown at the cinema in Barbados, searching for the secret to the American mystique.

He mimicked the language, the dances, the actions. Soon he could walk the walk and talk the talk. But still he couldn't get to America. He tried stowing away on a boat and was caught.

He applied for the farm workers program but was turned down. He gave up hope in the eighties when movies with black stars were replaced by Kung Fu at the local cinemas.

Why she never divorced him was a mystery. He kept writing her even after the letters started coming back unopened. Address Unknown. In between the letters and the many drunken nights spent cursing her, hating her, loving her…secretly, he found time to father three children by two different women. But he could not love either of them.

One evening in December of '89, a year ago, Sweets was jogging along Oistins beach, something he'd been doing since he was young. The woman sitting on a blanket on the sand staring at the white-capped water could not have looked more like Destine.

It was.

That night in her hotel room, she cried in his arms. Twenty years passed in one night, and just like in the movies love was born again. It was fate, he told her. They were meant to be together and he did not even think twice when she asked him if he still wanted to come to the States.

Fowl-Foot cursed him for being so donkey stupid. "After the way that woman piss on your head you going to the States to live wid she? Man, a jackass got more brains."

"I going. I deserve it for all the suffering. But don't think she getting off easy, you know," he boasted to his friend. "Wait til I get up there. I going to make she life hell until I feel she suffer as much as me."

"If that was me I wouldn't leave Barbados for all the flying fish in Tobago. Who? Not me. She would have to get down on she knees and kiss my feet first."

"Who would kiss them scaly things you got there?"

"Alright then. That is what I mean. She would have to kiss every one of these scales. You don't know what going happen when you get up there." Fowl-Foot charged. "You don't know what tricks she might pull. How you could trust that woman after what she do to you is a bare joke."

His last night on the island was spent like most of the others. Drinking. Shortly after sundown the tribe descended on his house like locusts on a fresh crop of corn: Sammy Boy, Fowl-Foot, Too-Tall, Sherwin, Chicken, Inches, Grant, Percy, Ducky, and a whole lot of strangers Percy dragged along from town. By morning, they'd all passed out from the gallons of white rum they'd consumed.

As salted as he was, he felt like a bridegroom on his way to the church when he boarded American Airlines flight 485. Minutes after the plane took off, he fell asleep and didn't wake up until he was on the ground again. He opened his eyes and smiled at the bearded woman next to him.

"Wait, what happen that the plane turn back?"

The woman sprang up, her face exploding in frustration. "Turn back? The plane ain't turn back. We in New York. And thank God!"

"Already? Jesus Christ, man, these planes does fly fast."

"Not fast enough. I never hear a man snore so hard in all me born days. I bet you wife dead. Only the dead could sleep through them horse snorts you was letting go. If I coulda open this window I woulda jump out the damn plane." The woman pushed past him and wobbled down the aisle.

Her outburst did little to faze him; neither did the long wait in the immigration room to have his picture taken for the green card. Nor did the rubber-faced customs officer who scrutinized his passport, for what seemed like an eternity.

"Your name is Othneil Straker?"

"Yes, but everybody does call me Sweets or Sweet Bread." He grinned at the youthful woman, whose chemically straightened hair was pulled back in a tight bun.

"What country are you coming from?"

"Bajan," he slurred.

"Bajan? Where is that?"

"Barbados." He stammered. "I mean, I from Barbados. But we does call weself Bajans."

"Do you have anything to declare?"

"Yes, sir, I mean, ma'am. I declare that I here to live with my wife of twenty-seven years."

The woman straightened her hunched shoulders.

"Do you have any alcohol?"

"Alcohol? I always got in my alcohol."

"Step over here, Mr. Straker. Unlock the black suitcase."

"This black one?"

She did not answer but gave him a look of hostility once reserved for white people on the New York subway, but now used more and more on immigrants who arrived with their trunks of poverty drunk with optimism.

Sweets fumbled in his pockets for the key finally giving up with a grin.

"I think I forget to bring the key."

The dark-skinned woman reached up and adjusted the gold chain around her neck. Then she opened a drawer behind her and withdrew a large bunch of keys on a thick silver ring. She examined the lock on the suitcase, then sifted through the keys before settling on a slim gold key. She inserted the key and twisted. The tiny lock squeaked open. Stepping back, she motioned to Sweet to unzip the suitcase.

Sweets abided with a involuntary burp, opening the bag to expose rows of rectangular packages wrapped in foil. The young woman picked up a package.

"What's in here?"

"Oh, that's my special sweet bread. My wife likes it. You know, there ain't nobody could make sweet bread to please she, but me. The secret is the coconut water I does use. I does mix it with a little white rum. And I does soak the raisins and grated coconut in it overnight. She don't know that. After that she does be ready for anything, you know what I mean?"

"Open it."

"Open it? Right now? Here? This is for my wife, you know."

"Do you want to go to jail?"

Sweets unfolded the silver foil, revealing shiny cut-rite paper which he unwrapped to display for the custom officer's unappreciative eyes, the most succulent looking coconut bread, baked an earthy brown, crisp at the edges, moist on top with raisins peeping out the sides, and topped with a cherry and sugared coconut.

She sniffed the bread. Then she broke one open. Out poured the smell of rum-soaked raisins, coconut, butter and vanilla essence.

"You got a boyfriend? I can leave one with you, yuh know," Sweets joked.

The agent did not answer. Her brown eyes closed slightly, and an odd expression bruised her face, as if she was stifling the urge to laugh at the thin man's cheek.

She made him open every one of the tightly wrapped packages. When she was satisfied there was nothing of contraband in his bags, with a wave of her hand and a broad smile, she sent him on his way.

By the time he stepped out into the night he was shivering. The thin tropical suit that had seemed so appropriate when he left his house was mere loincloth to ole man winter. The cold hit him like a two-by-four and the cobalt night wound about him, corkscrewing him to the ground. Dragging his suitcase, his eyes razed the crowd for a familiar face. The air was heavy and smelled of gasoline. Lights flashed before him. Police sirens screaming in the distance. People rushed past; faces moving with the blur of night.

Destine's sister, Alicia, picked him out in his brown suit and the brown fedora borrowed from Fowl-Foot. She approached, her eyes gleaming, her cheeks fat and saucy and handed him a thick gray wool coat.

"Where Destine?" He tried to ask.

The cold snatched the words from his mouth, smashing his teeth together like shack-shack seeds. Fearing his false teeth might fly out he stopped trying to speak and settled on a stupefied grin.

Alicia leaned close, her corpulence a sudden source of heat, and whispered into his ear. "Destine had to work. Good thing she ain't come, cause she would send your black ass back on the plane you come on. You smell like a dog."

He smiled and fell in behind her as they crossed the rain-slicked street to the parking lot.

sweets could tell that his stepdaughter didn't like him the minute he stepped through the door that first night. Soon afterward he arrived, she moved out with her little boy, Rae-Qwon. Not that Sweets minded one bit. Now he had Destine all to himself.

But in the face of Destine's indomitable zeal to recapture the lost years of their marriage he soon found he did not have the will nor the strength to deliver on his boast to make her life miserable. As if she'd been forewarned of his intentions, she launched a preemptive strike of such sensual and erotic force he was left to ponder if he'd died and gone straight to heaven. From the Victoria's Secret negligees she wore to bed, to the bubble baths she prepared, to shaving what was left of her pubic hair in the shape of an S for Sweet, she used every seductive technique she'd read in Essence. He was more than Shaft. He was now the star in his reality show.

Then Destine did something utterly remarkable. She confessed she'd come to Barbados looking for him.

"Two years ago my world started to collapse. I found out I had cancer. I'm in remission. A year now, thank God. It made me think about life in a whole new light. I prayed to God for guidance. And my mind keep focusing on you and how I treat you. My first and only true love. Is like God was trying to tell me something. That I needed to find my way back to me. The real me. All this loose living I been doing in New York. Partying. Spending money like it was sheep shite. Sleeping with all kinds of different men. Looking for what? What was I really getting? A one way ticket to the Devil. I realize you was the only man who ever really love me. When I get up here and got into school and realize what I could accomplish, I wanted to be free to experience all that New York had to offer. I sleep with more men than I care to remember and the truth is I never find nobody who really love me like you, who didn't want nothing from me but to treat me special."

That night he couldn't sleep. The thoughts were frightening. She say she sleep with more men than she care to remember. How many men that was? Twenty? Thirty? Forty? Could his Destine have slept with twenty or thirty men? In the middle of the night he woke shaking, so confused he couldn't find the bathroom, and peed all over the kitchen floor.

He drowned his anger in cheap beer and the tremor of the city's streets. He loved walking Brooklyn, especially after one of those long days sitting, waiting to be interviewed by the various employment agencies. These streets were louder, dirtier and more surreal than in the movies. New Yorkers walked with cynicism strapped like a six-gun to their hips but when they smiled: pure optimism. It was a strange paradox. Like his love for Destine. She'd done everything to hurt him, yet he loved her more than anything. Until now. Could he get over thirty or forty men?

a winter of high passion passed. Then life swooped in on April's back. Blossoms materialized out of thin air. Birds darted in and out of green leaves and cooed outside their window, urging them to make love in the morning. On the street, people had traded in their solemn winter skins for ripples of flesh and elastic smiles.

Saturday morning on Flatbush was carnival. Mini-van horns honking, reminding him of the ZR-vans back home. And so many people. So many different Caribbean accents. His head swelled listening to the storm of musical speech mingling with soca and reggae blasting from boom-boxes outside the stores as he strolled along the avenue.

Destine owned a rambling old house on East 22nd Street. Sweets was in the garden turning soil to plant more runners when Destine came home one hot July day. She set herself down on the porch with a weary sigh.

"Hi baby," Sweets called. She liked being called baby.

Destine smiled. She cocked her head and her gold earrings sparkled in the clear sunlight.

"You look so tired, baby," Sweets cooed.

"Tired? That don't begin to describe how I feel."

"You does work too hard. Why you got to work a double shift when we ain't even got no children to support. Is just the two of us."

Destine sighed. She ran her fingers along the edge of the carved wood of the railing.

"I think is time you get a job," she blurted.

Sweets straightened up.

"My family beginning to talk." Destine bowed her head. "Saying you don't like work."

"But you know that ain't true."

"I just want to shut them up. I got a friend working at Chase bank on Church. She tell me them looking for a courtesy guard."

friday morning. He looked at the uniform with pride. He liked his job. It was just as he expected, easy work. He hadn't gotten his first check yet, but it would be twice what he made in a month back home. He liked his uniform, too. But he wished he could wear a gun in a holster, like a real guard.

Carefully, he began to dress, not wanting to rumple his neatly pressed shirt. He polished his shoes one last time before stepping into them.

"You look so good in that uniform. You look like you could be a pilot," said a beaming half-naked Destine, who had just come out of the shower.

"Baby." He was holding her close now. Her hips wiggled as she absorbed the erotic charge of that word. Her wiggle gave him a tense erection. "Baby, tonight when you come home I going to put this big plane right in that hanger."

"Ooh, you so bad," Destine murmured. "I want you to keep on your uniform tonight when we make love. I been having this fantasy ever since I first see you in that uniform."

"Girl, you does got more fantasies than a writer. Is New York turn you like this?"

She sucked her teeth seductively. "You know you like it too."

He said nothing and turned to leave.

"Be careful, you hear," she said, as he went through the door.

He paused. "Every morning you going to tell me be careful? I ain't no child, you know. I know what I doing."

"I just don't want you to do nothing foolish. You know how you can be. Don't think that uniform give you the right to do anything stupid."

He balled his fists and went down the stairs.

He got to the bank ten minutes early. The manager arrived next, greeted him with a summery hello and opened the door. She was an elegant brown-skinned Antiguan with a grand smile and a broad straight back, the image of resolve and authority.

He took up his post near the front door at 9:00 sharp. Alert as always, his eyes followed every customer who came into the bank. His title might say "Courtesy Guard" but in his mind he was much more. He was John Wayne guarding Fort Knox. From time to time he walked around smiling, keeping things in order, discarding slips left half-used, restocking the various trays with forms.

Twelve-thirty was lunchtime. He ate two blocks away at the Jerk Place, a Jamaican restaurant, where he stuffed himself full of peas and rice and juicy oxtails. He bought a purple lollipop, which he put in his pocket for the walk home after work.

At 1:30 he returned to his post. On the stroke of two three men walked into the bank. Two were wearing suits, the other one Levi jeans, black long-sleeved shirt and black and white Puma sneakers.

The two suits strolled casually to the line of tellers at the far end of the bank. Sweets watched them with mild interest. The one in brown had pigeon toes, the one in gray was flat-footed. He glanced at Puma dawdling near the entrance and fingered the lollipop in his pocket. Suddenly, the suits pulled guns from under their jackets.

"Everybody on the floor! Now!" Gray-suit shouted.

Instant pandemonium. People fell to the floor screaming.

Shocked, Sweets remained standing.

Puma pulled a shiny silver pistol from the waist of his trousers.

"You heard the man! Face the floor. And don't move unless you got a death wish." He pointed the gun directly as Sweets' throat.

Sweets heard him, but his eyes were locked on the skinny face with the scraggly beard staring hotly at him.

I know this boy. I know this face. He look like Mavis Trotman first boy. Rodney. This could be Rodney?

He stared hard.

That is Rodney like shite. I used to cut he behind when he was a little boy back in Barbados. I used to cut his behind and send him home to his mother when I see him doing anything wrong. This can't be the same Rodney. His mother is a nice decent woman. That can't be Rodney. I remember when them leave Barbados. This is what he come to American to do?

"What the fuck? You deaf old man? I said on the floor!"

Sweets dropped to his knees. But the face of little bare-bottomed Rodney swimming through the khus-khus grass clogged his brain and he couldn't go any further.

Puma kicked him in the ribs and he fell forward on his hands.

"Now stay there, you old fart."

Sweets felt the blood rush to his head.

Man, that is Rodney like shite. That is Rodney. He ain't change one rass. He always used to run 'bout playing he is a bad-john. Never wanting to give up the bat when he get out. Always ready to curse people. Who the rass Rodney think he talking too? He forget how I used to cut his ass with my belt? He forget that?

Sweets got to his knees.

"You wanna die, old man?"

"Put down that gun Rodney. Is me, Sweet Bread. You don't remember me?"

Puma stared at him.

"Yes, man, look good. Is me, Sweet Bread. I know your mother good. I know you since you was a little boy. I used to give your mother money to buy sugar to make tea for you when you was small. You mother know what you doing, boy?"

Gray-suit shouted to Puma from across the room where he was waiting for the frightened teller to fill a plastic bag with money. "Shut that fucker up! Shoot him!"

Puma cocked the gun.

Sweets closed his eyes. He couldn't believe Rodney would shoot him.

Suddenly, the bank's doors crashed open.

"Police! Everybody on the floor!"

Sweets dropped, face down.

Puma spun around.

Shots rang out.

Puma fell.

His gun slid next to Sweets' face. The cold metal made him shiver and he shrank away. He opened his eyes and saw a pool of blood trickling toward him. He couldn't move. The blood flowed around him, along his cheek, into his hair.

when destine came home Sweets was packing his suitcase. He was still wearing the bloodied uniform. Before she could ask him what happened he whipped out the question that had baited his sleep all summer.

"How many men you think you sleep with?"

She hesitated. "I don't know. Maybe five. Six. Why?"

"I can't deal with that. I think I going back home."

GOING HOME IN CHAINS

passengers are *advised that large bags and backpacks are subject to random searches by law enforcement officials. All items must be attended at all times. Any item left unattended will be removed and subject to search by MTA police.*

Beneath the vaulted ceiling of Vanderbilt Hall, the announcement came over the public address system without a squawk. It was so clear and direct, that Tunde wondered why he'd never heard it before. Since the stepping up of security throughout the city after the 9-11 attacks, this simple caution must've echoed over his head as many times as he'd checked what little money he still had in the bank (always hoping there was more than he knew was there). Try counting the number of times he has been inside Grand Central Station in the last two years and you'd exhaust yourself.

Seriously. Had to be in the thousands. Yet tonight, at 8:09 P.M., was the first time he could remember hearing this warning.

Two hours later, he recalled the thought with the bitter taste of irony.

Still, irony was all in the timing, only useful to a writer, or an artist, eager to eke out a speck of meaning from an otherwise insignificant event. Tunde understood that irony had been wasted on him ever since the day he was born.

Extreme stress coupled with exhaustion after an 18-hour shift had all but finished him off for the day. He was so damn tired he didn't know what to do with himself. Not that he was complaining. No siree! After months of sporadic work, fortune delivered a pick to the city water tunnel project six weeks ago. And was he glad. With a leaky roof to fix, and getting word that his mother might need an operation soon, the opportunity to make some real money couldn't have come at a better time. Sure, it was dangerous work—at least 24 men had perished since construction began—but the money was too good to pass up. In the first week alone, with overtime, he cleared over $3,000 after taxes.

Another good thing about becoming a part of that strange underground world of the sandhogs was how quickly his mental state improved. It didn't completely cure the depression he'd been fighting ever since Astrid left, but he found himself smiling more than at any time during the previous year. The sandhogs all welcomed him without reservation, offering food and drink and advice from day one, treating him as if he was the prodigal son returned. And imagine his surprise when he discovered that a lot of Caribbean men were part of this select group.

Getting used to this new world, a world without sunlight, didn't take long. That was unusual, the others told him. Most people couldn't take the claustrophobia and ran from the job. But, most people weren't him, pursued by a tragic past or haunted by memories of what might've been. After what he'd been through in his life, spending his days with crazy workaholics was a veritable picnic by the sea with coconut ice-cream and sliced mango on top.

The abundant laughter and the presence and promise of tight bonds of friendship certainly helped him over the mild case of claustrophobia he suffered during the first week. He soon took to the underground like a vampire to a cloudy day. Except for weekends, he rarely saw the sun, and then very little of it. That was quite alright with him. One of the veterans, a sinewy guy of enormous strength, joked that it won't be long before Tunde lost his beautiful tan. "Look at me", the man joked, "When I started this job ten years ago, I was black, like you. Now, I'm a white man. I haven't seen the sun in ten years and my kids call me Santa because they only see me once a year. But I've never been happier. This hole transformed me. It will do the same to you. It will make you a better man."

Tunde regularly left his house before sun-up and returned at night. After such long shifts—sometimes 24 hours straight—he was so tired he could barely do anything but stretch out in his bed. He was accustomed to the grueling work now. In fact, he loved it. He couldn't wait to join his new friends under New York City every day. Whenever overtime was offered he jumped on it, not only because he needed the money, but time with the sandhogs was time away from certain realities he didn't want to face. The world of the sandhogs was a universe unto itself; and the men and women who inhabited it, a tribe like no other. They ate together, shared family histories and spoke frankly about their lives above. He knew how many lovers his co-workers had (though he wondered when they found the time for sex). Fathers and sons, and brothers and sisters worked alongside each other. One fella with a Phd in sociology became a sand-hog just to work with his sister. This one had a gambling problem. Another one couldn't keep out of the strip clubs. One woman, who brought crab cakes and crackers to work for lunch every day, was married to two men at the same time. She also had difficulty sleeping, an understandable condition given her marital confusion. But seriously, sleep problems were common among the sandhogs, and if for no other reason, this alone made Tunde a natural fit.

Even if you didn't become sleep deprived, the job took its toll. On everybody. You weren't getting the money without suffering. Just about every sandhog was on a second or third marriage. Alcoholism was a stud in their midst. Lately, Tunde had been experiencing bouts of temporary disorientation. At times, a sensation of disconnectedness from the rest of the world would hit him with such weight that he'd burst into tears. He was feeling that way tonight.

But more than anything, tonight he felt threatened. As if his life was in danger. Since he refused to get involved in that plot with the doctor, he's been looking over his shoulder at every turn. He suspected his house was being watched. When he left home this morning, two men sitting in a car across the street quickly sped off when he approached them. Going to the police was out of the question. They would want to know about his relationship with the doctor. If he told them about the plot, he would most surely be arrested. What a mess!

The presence of army personnel patrolling the station was the only thing that kept Tunde from removing his jacket and laying it down on the floor to rest his head for the 30 minutes he had to wait for the next train to Mount Vernon.

Keeping his leaden eyelids open was becoming impossible. He had to keep moving, find something else to occupy his mind. Hunching his shoulders, he hobbled along, scraping his soles on the marble surface, almost running into a group of people who'd stopped to stare at the ceiling. With a curiosity born of fatigue and boredom, he followed their gaze. The boring laser light show underway was more apt to thrust him further into the sleep's bosom than keep him awake so he lumbered on.

He reached Grand Central Market and went inside. Of the many things he loved about Grand Central Station, this market had to be one of his favorites. Now here was a place you could let your mind wander. Food did that to him. Opened up his imagination. Not much chance of falling asleep in here.

The glorious varieties of food found in Grand Central Market thrilled his eyes and on most days, soothed his mind. His delight in food was probably the product of childhood summers spent helping out in aunt Velda's cook-shop in Bridgetown. After doing his chores, which varied from washing carrots to peeling potatoes to scraping bun-bun from pots, he got to sample everything she cooked. From cou-cou and macaroni pie to black pudding and pickled pig's feet. And how could he forget the pone and coconut puffs and turnovers which she stuffed into his bag for him to take home.

Grand Central Market had almost anything edible you could imagine. Okay, so you wouldn't find anything to match his aunt's cou-cou and steamed flying fish, but how often does the universe produce a Mozart? What you will find is a shop called World Edibles which sold a variety of fresh fish imported from all parts of the world. Now, how sweet was that?

Fresh and pre-cooked fish and meat. Cheeses from every corner of the globe. A hundred varieties of freshly baked bread. All types of sausages. Green olives. Black olives. Varieties of pasta dishes that made his mouth water every time he looked. Spices. Exotic fruits. Chocolate. Coffee from as far away as Kenya. Name it and you'd find it in Grand Central Market.

Leaving the market, he walked back into the great hall. He dodged a lean woman motoring to catch a train. Her flailing handbag caught him a blow on the left side of his head.

He turned and spat in anger. "Bitch!"

But, moving with unbridled speed, she had already submerged herself in the large throng swelling behind him.

More and more he was beginning to believe that white people didn't really see him when they walked. Or if they did, they expected him to move out of their way, or stop to let them pass if it appeared their trajectories might intersect.

A few weeks ago he resolved to quit doing that: stopping to let them by, that is. If they pretended they didn't see him, then he'd walk as though he didn't see them either. The first day he tested his newfound courage, a large woman talking on her cell phone ran smack into him. She outweighed him by about eighty pounds and the force of her blow *catspraddled* him on the ground. Looking up from the vantage point of a squashed ant he saw that she was black. After helping him up and asking if he was alright, she offered to buy him coffee, which he declined. The next day he went back to dodging everybody. Black, White and Indifferent.

He turned his attention to the bakery snuck in between tracks 17 and 18, thinking one of their delicious apple turnovers would be just the thing to make him forget his troubles. Halfway across the threshold of the pastry shop he realized something was wrong. He was walking too freely, his body too light.

His bag!

He'd left his bag against the wall near gate 30.

He dashed back across the Great Hall, dodging people with the skill of a halfback. From ten yards away, he saw two soldiers in army fatigues, with guns slung over their shoulders standing over his bag. Next to them was a policewoman holding a leashed dog. The dog sniffed at his bag and barked.

Tunde skidded to a stop. This couldn't be good. With a split second to decide if he was going to turn and walk away as fast as possible or try to repossess his bag, he was a split second too late.

One of the soldiers looked his way. Noticing Tunde's flustered demeanor, the soldier began walking with earnest toward Tunde, his rifle raised. "Come here."

Tunde did not move.

"I'm talking to you." The soldier pointed his rifle at Tunde's chest.

Fright charged through Tunde, staking him to the spot. Even if he tried, he couldn't move. The policewoman with the dog marched over to join the soldier pointing the rifle. The other soldier guarded the bag while talking animatedly on his walkie-talkie.

The soldier's gun was now inches away from Tunde's nose. He was slightly taller than Tunde's five-eight; a scrubby fellow with dour eyes. And very young. He couldn't have been long out of high school. Freckles black-peppered his face. But the shine on his gun was what really got Tunde's attention. The soldier held the weapon confidently, with an alertness that made Tunde wince, though his nice southern accent made the youngster seem almost pleasant.

"That your bag, Sir?"

Tunde nodded.

The admission seemed to make the soldier agitated. He brought the gun even closer to Tunde's face. Tunde could smell the metal, and the oil used to clean it.

The soldier glared. "Why were you about to run?"

Tunde did not answer. He was afraid that if he opened his mouth this overzealous soldier might make him eat the nozzle.

The policewoman, now standing next to the soldier, was short with rounded shoulders and a man's mouth; she reminded Tunde of a cousin who sold her house so she could get money to go to England to see Westminster Abbey.

She jabbed his chin with the walkie-talkie, "What's your name?" The black gloves fitted snugly and the walkie-talkie looked like a club in her tiny hands.

"My name?"

The dog barked.

The policewoman removed her dark glasses revealing pinched eyes. "A problem with your hearing?"

"What?"

The soldier jerked the rifle upward. "Come with us."

"I don't understand," Tunde mumbled.

The policewoman's voice was brusque and impatient. "What the fuck don't you understand about: come with us? Are you retarded?" She stepped forward, her eyes dark as coal. "Turn around."

The dog barked twice.

Tunde stood still, giddy with shock. "Have you ever seen Westminster Abbey?"

The policewoman froze, then leaned her head toward him. "Fuck that you say?"

"I'm sorry," Tunde fumbled.

"Did you just insult me?" Her voice, scraped of its pitch, was flat and icy.

"I'm sorry," Tunde apologized again. "I don't know what I was saying."

The space around him suddenly darkened. He looked around. A gang of police officers, all dressed in black, had surrounded him. This large ring of cops now had Tunde completely cordoned off from passersby.

"I didn't mean to cause no trouble," He heard himself say. Words started to spill rapidly now. "I went to get a turnover and forgot it. I didn't mean to cause any trouble. I wouldn't do it again. I have to go home now. Please. Let me go home. I'm so tired. I want to sleep."

"Turn around," the policewoman snapped. She clamped a gloved hand on Tunde's wrist even before he could reply. With a violent twist she jerked him around. Sharp pain exploded in his shoulder socket. He began to struggle. Immediately, several more tentacles latched onto him. Someone put his head in a lock. Then everything went black.

lights brighter than a morning sun. The shock of it all closed his eyes again. He kept them that way as he tried to clear his head. What had happened? Was he dreaming again?

OK. When I open my eyes again I'll be home in my bed. It'll be morning. Time to get ready for work. I'll get up, wash my hands and face, then go to the kitchen and put four eggs to cook, and while those are cooking I'll take a quick shower. Very hot water. That'll wake me up. Then I'll eat two of the eggs with a warm ginger beer to help break up the gas. After that, I'll wrap the other two in foil and then go to get dressed.

Tunde opened his eyes. After blinking several times, he closed them against the reality that was quickly gaining momentum. This was not a dream. This was not his house. This was not his bed. He was handcuffed to a gurney that was hard as rock. The room was cold and the blinding lights hurt his eyes. Everything was blurry. There were people around him. Strangers. He could hear them, but couldn't make out any faces. Still fighting the realness of this experience, he kept blinking and blinking, hoping against hope that it would all go away.

Someone with a heavy voice spoke. "Hey there, buddy."

Tunde decided that the man wasn't talking to him. Then he felt a huge hand envelop his head, squeezing his skull hard, as if it was trying to make his ears touch each other.

"How're you feeling, buddy?"

Tunde tried to sit up.

The hand aggressively pushed him back onto the bed.

"You don't move unless I tell you to. Understand?"

Tunde did not respond.

"Nod your head if you understand. Do you speak English?"

Tunde nodded.

"What's your name?"

Tunde had to think a minute. He didn't know why, but his name wasn't where it would normally be. His name? Must've been the blow to the head.

"You don't know your name?

"My name's Tunde," he said.

"Tunde?"

"Tunde Ham?"

"You asking or you telling?" the man said.

"Tunde Ham."

"You sure?" There was more than a snatch of mockery in his voice.

Tunde said, "Yes, I'm sure. My name is Tunde Ham."

"You Muslim?"

Tunde shook his head.

"You sure you don't want to think about that for a while?"

Tunde nodded.

"You do or you don't?"

"I ain't Muslim," Tunde stressed.

"Where're you from?"

"Mount Vernon."

"Is that where were you born?"

"Guyana, but…" Tunde paused.

"But what?"

"I grew up in Barbados."

"And now you live in Mount Vernon?"

Tunde nodded.

"So, you name is Tunde Ham, you were born in Guyana, you grew in Barbados and now you live in Mount Vernon. Is that correct."

Tunde nodded.

"That makes you what? A Guyanese-Bajan-American?"

Tunde didn't respond. This man was trying to make fun of him for reasons Tunde couldn't understand. But he was impressed that the man knew that people from Barbados were sometimes called Bajans. He probably had a daughter who listened to Rihanna.

"Did you, by accident or intentionally, stop off in Africa on your long journey?" the man added. "Perhaps a Bin Laden camp in the Sudan or somewhere?"

The laughter in the man's voice was obvious now, and Tunde heard the others chuckle along.

"Tell us about the bag, Tunde," the man said.

"What bag?"

Tunde tried to sit up again. The hand pushed him down with even greater force, jolting his neck.

"What did I tell you? I told you not to move."

The man cleared his throat, and even that sounded menacing. "Tell us about the bag you left on the floor in Grand Central."

Tunde blinked. Ah, focus. The rows of hooded lamps above his head were housed in bright orange cones. Peripheral vision returning. To his left he could make out two men in suits. He couldn't see their faces, but he could smell their stinky cologne. He raised his head slightly. Not enough to incur the wrath of the tyrannical hand behind him, he hoped, but enough to see who was in front of him. Several people directly at the foot of the bed.

The man behind him spoke again. "Are you listening? I wanna know about the bag. Why did you leave that bag?"

"I didn't leave it. I forgot it."

"You forgot it?"

"Yeah."

The man said, "Was that a test run?"

"A test run?"

"To see how long it would take us to spot it."

The questions puzzled Tunde, but he was more concerned with the handcuffs pinching his wrists. "Why am I in handcuffs?"

"Answer the question."

"They hurt."

The man clamped his paw on Tunde's head and squeezed hard. "Answer the goddamn question."

The pressure went straight through Tunde's skull making his teeth hurt. If the man squeezed any harder his fingers would meet in Tunde's brain for sure.

"What question?" Tunde pleaded.

"Was that some kind of test run?"

"I don't know what you mean by a test run. A test run for what?"

"What do you do for a living?"

"I'm a sandhog."

"A sandhog?"

"Yes."

"You're working water tunnel number three?"

"Yes."

The man reduced the force of his grip but still held Tunde's head firmly. "How did you get a job working on that project?"

Tunde was quiet. He didn't want to get Brother Khalil in any trouble.

"I'm losing my patience, my friend. You don't want that. When I ask you a question, answer me. Is that clear?"

Tunde nodded.

"How did you get a job on that project?"

"A friend."

"What's his name?"

"Ronald Johns. He's the foreman."

"If I find out you're not telling me the truth. Are you telling me the truth?"

"Yes, I'm telling the truth."

The man smoothed the bald spot on the crown of Tunde's head with the gentleness of a doting mother, then took his hand away. "How long have you been working on that project?"

"Not long. A few months. My hands hurt. Can I sit up now?"

A door opened. Warm air flowed into the room. Tunde heard a boot scratch the floor. And then there was whispering. He smelled hot cheese and tomato sauce and assumed someone had brought pizza.

"Are you hungry?" a man said.

This voice was nasal and soft. Friendlier. Definitely not the voice of The Hand.

Someone unshackled him. Tunde looked up. The face hovering over him could only be described as tomato-colored. Tunde had never seen anyone that red. It was shocking. Either, the man had a bad suntan, or he'd borrowed the Shikami mask from a Noh theater group. Then Tunde noticed his hands, which were the size of baseball gloves. Those had to be the hands that had been kneading his head. Made sense that someone with hands that big would have an odd face.

Tunde sat up. His head began to spin and panic clutched him with terrifying force. He closed his eyes and felt everything floating away.

"You okay?" The man with the nasal voice.

The swoon passed and Tunde opened his eyes once more. Better. He was able to focus now.

The room was about 7 feet square. No windows. The way voices echoed meant that the walls were thick. Two of the three men were square and solidly built. The man with the oversized hands had dark grainy eyes and was taller than the other two by a good six inches

"I bet you're hungry," he said to Tunde. "Look what we've got. Trust me when I tell you this. Many places make the claim, but this is the best pizza in the city. Even better than Ray's, which, frankly, is way overrated, not to mention overpriced. I mean, do you think I could afford a whole pie from Ray's on my expense account?"

In a halting voice Tunde said, "Where am I?"

"Come on. Let's eat first."

Tunde became more alarmed. "What time is it? I have to go to work."

"Relax, my friend"

"Relax? What do you mean relax? Why are you holding me?"

"Fella, you're in big trouble. Just relax."

"How can I relax? I don't know where I am. I don't know why you people are holding me. And why're you saying I'm in big trouble? For what?"

"You people?"

"What did I do? I didn't do anything wrong."

"You left a bag in a corner in Grand Central Station. We want to know why."

"It's just a bag. And I already told you. I forgot it."

The man's eyes deepened. "You and I both know it's not just the bag."

"What you mean it's not just the bag?"

"We've got some questions and we want answers."

"About what? My bag?"

"About your life?"

"About my life? What do you mean?"

The man handed Tunde a slice of pizza on a yellow paper plate "Come on, let's eat. We've got all day. And then some. It's hard to talk when you're hungry."

Tunde looked at the pizza and knew there was no point trying to eat it. The chances of anything getting past his throat was as good as someone off the street wandering into the white house. He gave the plate back.

When they asked him to stand up, he couldn't. The pain from the tangled knot in his gut shot all the way down the back of his legs and he collapsed to the floor. Someone brought a wheelchair and they lifted him into it.

by van, they took him on a trip that lasted about 2 hours. Tunde tried to peer outside, but the thick dark tint at the windows made it impossible to see anything. The second they stopped the back door flew open. Men in dark uniforms carrying sub-machine guns stood waiting. It was the kind of welcoming party Tunde would never have imagined.

One of the three guards inside the van ordered him to stand. Tunde did so, though his legs were still rubbery.

With the precision of a well-rehearsed dance, they whisked him inside the flat gray building through a side entrance before he had a chance to get his bearings. He had no idea where he was.

They kept him in a darkened room. No light. No sound. No chairs. No chance of escape. He lay down on the cold floor and quickly fell asleep. He dreamed that Luis Posada had visited Barbados to lay a wreath at the monument to the people he killed on board Cubana 455.

tunde awoke with fire in his bladder. Or was it his balls? It was hard to tell because his whole body seemed to be stricken with a crippling pain. The dream he had of Luis flashed into him mind. Would he ever stop dreaming about that man?

And though the dream remained fuzzy he sensed that it'd been a different kind of dream this time; for gone was the tortuous clenching of his heart that always attended the remembering of his dreams of Luis. Even in his present predicament a smile opened on his face. Could it be? Was he finally free of this anguish that had long dulled his sleep? Was this the release he'd sought for so long? If so, how ironic for it to happen now.

Tunde rubbed his eyes and then opened them, slowly letting light seep in. He tried to move but the pain was so intense he could not get himself in an upright position. If he didn't pee right away he would surely burst into a geyser.

He crawled to the door and began banging as hard as he could. Nobody came. He banged and banged and banged

until his knuckles hurt. Five minutes later he was still banging to the unresponsive audience he knew was watching on
closed-circuit TV. No longer able to bear the pain playing
ping-pong between his bladder and his balls, he crawled to a
corner in the back of the room and unzipped his pants,
urinating on the floor with a loud sigh.

His relief was short-lived. The door flew open as his
triumphant *aaaghh* reached its zenith. A dynamic duo who
looked like they'd just escaped from a superhero comic
book charged into the room. Same height. Same broad face
and square chin. They even wore the same color suits. They
were clearly twins, unless Tunde was seeing double. The
twins pinned him against the wall and stuffed his wrists into
handcuffs.

"Nasty muthafucker," cursed one.

They hustled him off down a narrow empty hallway to
another room. This room was smaller than the previous one,
but it came fully furnished: a table and two chairs, which was
really all it could hold. They forced Tunde into one of the
chairs and stepped back glaring at him in unison. For a
second Tunde expected to see laser beams come shooting out
of their eyes.

A full minute later the man with the red face made a
dramatic entrance chewing gum so vigorously that the veins at
his temples bulged. "Where the fuck do you think you are?"

"I had to go." Tunde said.

"You had to go?"

"I had to go," Tunde cried. "What was I supposed to do? I
had to go. I know you heard me and saw me banging on the
door. Why didn't you come?"

"We thought you were drumming to show how happy and excited you were to be with us," one of the twins said.

The three inquisitors laughed together.

The man with the red face sat in the chair opposite Tunde and shrugged. "Hey, you had to go. I can understand that. Is there anything else you want? A beer maybe? A cigarette? mango?"

"I want to call a lawyer," Tunde said quietly. If he was in serious trouble as they claimed, this was America and he still had rights.

"You want to call a lawyer?" one of the twins mocked.

"Yes. This is America. I have a right to call a lawyer."

"And you think we're going to let you call a lawyer?"

"You have to. It's my right."

"You, my friend, are being treated as an enemy combatant. You have no rights."

"A what?"

The three men looked at each other. The man with the red face nodded. One of the twins left the room.

"How am I an enemy combatant?" Tunde pressed. But his voice faltered. He'd heard that term used in relation to terror suspects captured in the Iraq war who were shipped to Guantanamo. Were they trying to say that he was a terrorist? The room became silent. The tiny eyes of the man with the red face quickly became remote, the nuances of amusement and jest having been erased as if by magic.

The man who'd left the room returned with Tunde's black canvas bag. He plopped it down on the desk in front of Tunde.

"I think it's time we introduce ourselves," the man with the red face said. "My name is Captain Jericho. I'm with the

Department of Homeland Security. That's Lieutenant Alvin
Petersen, and Lieutenant Dan Petersen. They're brothers.
They look alike because they're twins." Jericho looked deep
into Tunde's eyes. "Traces of explosives were found in your
bag. We also found dynamite caps at your home. Now, do
you want to continue to fuck with us or will you tell us the
truth? Either way, you goose is cooked, my friend. Now how
do you wanna eat it? Let's begin at the beginning, shall we?
What's your name?"

Tunde was too stunned to speak.

Jericho seized Tunde's jaw in his thick paw and squeezed.
"What is your name?"

"I already told you my name."

"I'm not going to ask again," Jericho menaced.

"Tunde Ham."

"Are you Muslim?"

"No. I told you before. How many times do I have to tell
you no?"

"What were the caps for?"

"What caps? I don't know nothing 'bout no caps.
Somebody else put them there."

"Did you plan to blow up the water tunnel?" Lt. Al
Petersen asked.

"You must be crazy."

"The longer you deny it, the worse it's going to be," Jericho
threatened.

"I'm a hard worker. I love my job. Why would I blow up
the tunnel?"

"We've been watching you, Mr. Ham," Lt. Dan Petersen
said.

"Watching me? What do you mean?"

"We've had our eyes on you," chimed Lt. Alvin Petersen.

"You've got to be joking," Tunde said. "I don't believe you. Why would you be watching me. I haven't done anything."

"We got an anonymous tip about two weeks ago," Jericho said.

"A tip. About me? From who?"

Jericho spread his fingers out on the table. "Anonymous shall remain just that."

"It can't be anonymous," Tunde said desperately. "I don't believe you. You're making all this up. Why're you doing this to me?"

You want to help yourself, Tunde? Stop wasting our time. You're not leaving here. So, talk to me. I'm a very good listener, you know. And who knows, if your story excites me, I might even let you up on the roof for a little fresh air. What were you doing with dynamite caps in your home?"

"I don't know nothing about no caps."

"Have you ever used dynamite?" Jericho asked.

Tunde paused. "Yes. A long time ago."

"Where?"

"In construction. In Guyana."

"Is that where you got training in explosives?"

"Who told you I got training in explosives," Tunde said.

"Answer my fucking question," Jericho fumed.

"I don't have any training in explosives," Tunde said after a long pause.

"That's why they chose you, isn't it?" Jericho asked.

"Why who chose me?"

"Your Muslim brothers."

"I ain't got no brothers."

"Do you know a Brother Khalil?"

Tunde paused. A voice in his gut was talking to him. Should he tell them the truth? "Yes, I know Brother Khalil."

"Did he try to recruit you into his organization?" Jericho asked.

"Not really."

"What is not really?"

"He's a friend. We talked about all kinds of things."

"Including joining his organization."

"What organization? I don't know nothing 'bout joining no organization," Tunde said.

"So he never tried to get you to become a Muslim?"

"He might've mentioned it."

"Have you ever prayed with him?" Jericho asked.

"What does praying have to do with anything?"

"Answer the question."

"No, I've never prayed with him."

"Are you sure of that?"

"I don't remember praying with him," Tunde said.

"Tell us about Cuba," Jericho said.

"Cuba?"

"You spent some time in Cuba, didn't you?"

Tunde paused. The voice in his gut was talking to him again. What didn't they know about him? "Yes, I was in Cuba a very long time ago. I don't remember much about it now."

"When was that? When were you in Cuba?" Jericho asked.

"Way back in the seventies. It was a long time ago."

"What did you do in Cuba?"

"I went to study medicine."

"So, you're a doctor?"

"No. I didn't finish."

"Was it because of what happened on flight four fifty-five?" Jericho asked.

He should've known that if they knew about him being in Cuba, they would also know about 455.

"Cubana flight four fifty-five," Jericho pressed. "You remember that flight don't you?"

Tunde bowed his head. He didn't want to talk about 455.

Jericho grabbed Tunde's chin and raised his head. "Look at me! Do you remember Cubana flight four fifty-five?"

Tunde nodded. How could he forget.

"Tell us about that flight."

"What do you want to know?"

"You were arrested on suspicion of bombing that plane."

Tunde tried to hold back the anger welling inside him, but couldn't. "You all know who bombed that plane. It wasn't me."

He wished they would leave him alone now that they'd stirred up the bones of CU455. His first love had died on that plane and these three men were the last people on earth with whom he wanted to talk about Jenny.

Jericho spoke softly now. "Who bombed the plane?"

"You all know."

"Tell us who you think did it."

"The CIA bombed that plane. And you know it better than me."

"Is that why you wanted to blow up Grand Central Station? Are you angry because you think the CIA bombed that plane and killed your girlfriend?"

they interrogated him for days. Maybe weeks. He lost track of time. They tried to get him to admit that he was a communist. That he was an Islamist sympathizer. That he hated the CIA. That he hated America. That he hated apple pie. That he hated his mother. That he hated himself.

Why did he have Malcolm X's speeches on his computer?

Why did he have all those pictures of Grand Central Station?

Why did he drink coffee from Kenya?

Why wasn't he married?

How often did he masturbate?

He stopped answering their questions until they threatened to throw his ass in Guantanamo.

"Can I have some water?" Tunde asked Jericho.

Jericho nodded to Dan Peterson who left the room and returned with a glass of water. It was brownish-looking, as if it'd been scooped from a river. Tunde took a sip. It tasted like mercury.

Jericho tried his most persuasive voice. "You're a very angry man, Tunde. I can feel it. Can't you feel it, Lieutenant?"

Al Petersen smirked. "Hell, yeah. It's like a force field. He's so angry, I think our ancestors can feel it."

Jericho said, "Who're you angry with, Tunde? Let me help you. Talk to me. Get it off your chest. You will feel much better. Guantanamo is not a pretty place. It ain't paradise. It ain't a day at the beach in Barbados, I can tell you that. Tell me your story, Tunde. You don't want to end up at Guantanamo. And that's where you'll end up if you keep this up. We've all got a story we want to tell the world. I understand that. Hell, when I get out of this crazy job I plan to write a book. Tell my own sad story. Every ex-government official is doing it. Why shouldn't I get rich, too? Unburden yourself, Tunde. You'll feel better."

Tunde took a deep breath and closed his eyes. He wanted to relax. He wanted the muscles in his neck and back to stop twitching. He wanted his hands to stop shaking. He wanted to lie down and go to sleep.

"I used to be very angry. I admit that. But I've gotten better. I'm not so angry anymore. I like who I am now. But if you had to live my life you would've been angry too. I used to be angry at my father. But I'm over that. He was American, you know. Did you know that? Yup, born right here in the U. S. of A. But I bet you know that. You seem to know everything else about me. But, here's something no amount of digging or surveillance could possibly tell you. And that's how much I loved Jenny. You could never know how I felt about her in my heart. You could never knowthe part of me that died with her on Cubana four fifty-five."

He'd tried not to think about that day. Or the days and weeks that followed. But he had come to realize there was no running away from the memories. The love of his life had died on that plane. Five of his good friends went down that day. It happened a Tuesday evening. The next day it was all over the news.

BARBADOS DAILY NEWS
Wednesday October 7, 1976
Terror over Barbados' Waters
By Denis Samuel

Flight CU-455 took off from Guyana and landed, first in Trinidad, and then in Barbados. At 17:17, it took off from Barbados for Jamaica, the penultimate scheduled stop on its way to Havana.

But it never made it to Jamaica. Nine minutes after takeoff from Barbados' Seawell airport, a bomb exploded in one of the aircraft's rear lavatories. The leased DC-8 had reached an altitude of 20,000 feet, 16,000 feet short of cruising altitude. The captain, Wilfredo Pérez, radioed the control tower: "We have an explosion aboard, we are descending immediately! There is a fire on board! Requesting immediate landing! This a total emergency! Repeat! Total emergency! Immediate permission to land!"

A second bomb exploded in another of the lavatories. The plane went into an immediate and rapid descent. The pilots tried to return the aircraft to Seawell Airport, but realizing that a successful landing was impossible, it appears that they changed course and took the plane back towards the Atlantic Ocean.

All 48 passengers and 25 crew aboard the plane died: 57 Cubans, 11 Guyanese, and five

North Koreans. Among the dead were all 24
members of the 1975 national Cuban fencing
team that had just won all the gold medals
in the Central American and Caribbean
Championships. Many were teenagers.

The 11 Guyanese passengers included 18 and
19-year-old medical students, and the young
wife of a Guyanese diplomat.

Barbadian police have reportedly taken a
young Guyanese-Barbadian into custody for
questioning as a person of interest in this
act of terror over Barbados.

Unofficial transcript of the interrogation of
Tunde Ham, compiled from an eye-witness account
given to reporter Denise Samuel of the Barbados
Observer by a news source within the Royal
Barbados Police.

October 10. 1976. Barbados. 3 days after CU 455
bombing.

A dimly lit room in the basement of CID
(Criminal Investigations Department). Three men
are crammed into the tiny room. The broad-
shouldered youngster sitting at a square table
has the red eyes of sleeplessness. He rubs his
eyes as the other men, dressed conservatively
in long-sleeve shirts, ties and slacks, examine
documents extracted from a large Manila enve-
lope. One of the men holds a black billy club.

                    1ST INTERROGATOR
Why did you get off the plane, Tunde?

                         TUNDE
I told you. I wanted to see my mother.

                    2ND INTERROGATOR
What's her name?

                         TUNDE
Veronica Whitfield.

                    1ST INTERROGATOR
Is that your real name? Tunde Ham?

                         TUNDE
Yes.

                    1ST INTERROGATOR
Why did you leave your suitcase on the plane?

                         TUNDE
It was supposed to come off in Barbados with
me. But they forgot, I suppose.

                    2ND INTERROGATOR
Who forgot?

                         TUNDE
The baggage people.

                    2ND INTERROGATOR
You had a ticket to Cuba.

                         TUNDE
I changed it at the airport to get off
Barbados.

                    2ND INTERROGATOR
Why you decide to change your flight?

                         TUNDE
I wanted to see my mother. I told you.

                    1ST INTERROGATOR
Don't lie to us, you little shite.
[Smacks Tunde on the head with the club.]
Who do you work for?
               [Tunde begins to cry.]

                    2ND INTERROGATOR
All of a sudden you're crying like a sissy?
You blow up a plane full of people and you're
crying? Don't try that shite. It ain't going
move us. Do you work for the CIA?

                         TUNDE
I'm a student.

                    1ST INTERROGATOR
How much they pay you to blow up that plane?

                        TUNDE
I didn't blow up no plane.

                    1ST INTERROGATOR
Stop lying to us, you piece of shite!
        [Smacks him on the head with club.]
We going to swing your skinny rass from the
gallows.
        *[A superintendent, in uniform, enters
        the room. He has a serious face. The
        other two men stand at attention. He
        whispers something to the two men and
        they quickly leave. He looks at Tunde
        and smiles.]*

                     SUPERINTENDENT
How're you doing, Mr. Ham?

                        TUNDE
Why you all got me in here like this? I ain't
do nothing.

                     SUPERINTENDENT
I know that. And I'm here to apologize.
You're free to go.
        [Tunde doesn't move.]
Did you hear me? You're free to go. We caught
the real bombers. Two men were arrested in
Trinidad. They confessed.
        [Tunde stands up.]
One question before you go? What kind of name
is Tunde Ham?

"I came here to see my father who was in the hospital on his deathbed. I came here hoping he'd still be alive so I could say all the things I've been holding in my bosom. My father was born in Boston. He moved to Trinidad and brought the Black Power movement. The Trinidad government chased him out and he went to Barbados where he met my mother. The Barbados government chased him out because all his Black Power rants were making the white people scared. He took my mother with him to Guyana where I was born.

"He treated her bad. Like shit. My mother had to run and leave Guyana because my father terrorized her. Ran back to Barbados with nothing. We stayed with my aunt and her son, Mort. He was the only friend I had for a long time. His father drove a taxi and would take all of us on drives on Sunday afternoon. Barbados is beautiful and I had fun growing up there. My mother worked in factories and saved enough money to buy a little house. I did well in school and got a scholarship to study in Cuba. But I never forgot what my father done.

"When I got the word that he was dying and wanted to see me, I didn't want to come at first. And then I saw that it was my chance to tell him all the things I had on my mind. So, yes, I came here an angry man. But when I got here he was already gone. He died as my plane was touching down at JFK. Once more, I had to keep my anger bottled up. Had I not met Brother Khalil I don't know what I would've done with my anger.

"I met Brother Khalil in the park. He was talking to a group of people one evening and I stopped to listen. He invited me up to Harlem where he introduced me to his brothers from the Black Muslim faith. He thought I was African because of my name. The Muslim brothers got me a job in construction. And they helped me find an apartment. Small, but clean and nice. And they counseled me on the ways of America. How natural it is for every other race to treat black people like they have no worth. How America's culture of materialism is destroying the black man's soul. How it keeps the black man down. They thought they were telling me something I didn't know. But this wasn't nothing that I didn't know. I'd read all the books back home. *Black Like Me, Manchild in the Promise Land.* Malcolm X's autobiography. I read them all. I knew what America was. I ain't had no problem with America. But all they try I refuse to convert to Islam. And that made them vex. So I stopped going 'round them.

"I moved to Brooklyn and got work on a building that was getting repaired. After that, there was no turning back for me. I did such a good job that the contractor hired me for another job in Queens. People on the job started to take notice of me. They realized that I was not only good at construction, but I had good brains, too. I could've told them that I went to one of the best schools in Barbados, but I didn't. I could've told them that I got a scholarship to study medicine. I didn't tell them that stuff because I knew they wouldn't care. All they cared about was that I got the job done. I did that so well, they make me a foreman. I was making good money. I met a woman and I bought a house in Mount Vernon.

"But then nine-eleven changed everything. Jobs became scarce. When people heard my name, even though I tell them that I wasn't Muslim they find excuses not to hire me. I didn't work for a long time. The woman I was living with left me. But then I got a break. I got that job working with the sandhogs. A fella from Barbados was in the union. I know him through the cricket club up there in Mount Vernon. He heard 'bout me as a hard worker. And he worked it out for me. See, that is how people suppose to live. Not everybody turning on everybody. That is how people suppose to live. People should help each other.

"And then I met this doctor from Queens one day at cricket match. His son was on Cubana four fifty-five when it was bombed. I told him I got off the plane in Barbados. A stroke of luck. He told me that the damn thing still haunts him. You don't know the half of it, I say. I still have trouble sleeping. Then he tells me how he's been following that case for years. His obsession. He mentioned that Nightline did a program recently on the bombing. Not too long ago. He said that he can't understand why the United States won't deport that man, Luis Posado, who was responsible for killing some of our brightest scholars in the Caribbean. You think that is fair? That he should get asylum after killing so many people?

"But that is how life is. That Luis Posada fella, he was working for the CIA for many years. He worked for Oliver North in El Salvador. He killed all kinds of people. Bomb hotels and thing. Yet, he here in the United States. He here free as a bird. Why it is that he free? The president of the United States, George Bush, say that no country should harbor terrorists. Why is it that he free? That man blow up a plane that kill innocent Guyanese. All those innocent people he killed. And he walking 'bout free in Miami. And then my doctor friend said we should kill this man. This Luis Posada. We should make a bomb and blow up his house in Miami. And at first, it make sense. This Luis fella deserved to die. And I started looking for a way to make a bomb. And then I say, no. I really ain't about nothing so. I'm a peaceful man. I just forgetful, that is all, but I'm a peaceful man. You all arrest because I forgetful. For forgetting my bag in Grand Central for a few minutes. What you all don't know is that I love that place. I worked on that place when it was being fixed up. I work hard to make it look beautiful again. And you all think I would blow it up?"

"What is his name? This doctor friend of yours?" Jerico said.

They decided to send him back to Barbados after he gave them the doctor's name. When the deportation order was handed to him, he didn't even read it. He really didn't care as long as they let him sleep.

The day came and he was escorted to a plane along with several other men. Like him, they all had chains binding their ankles and wrists. The other men had trouble walking. Not him. He approached it as if he was walking in the confined space in the water tunnel. There, you had to take small steps. He watched as others lost their balance trying to walk too fast. He took his time. The plane wasn't going anywhere without him. As the plane taxied, he looked out the window. One last look at America. Gray clouds all around. Looked like snow. Just like the day he arrived.

Then he closed his eyes. It had been a long time since he slept.

This story is adapted from a novel-in-progress called: *Dreaming of Luis: A Bomber's Tale of Unyielding Love*

COURT JESTERS

if you couldn't take a joke you didn't last long in the
Palace. Plain and simple. Rum drinking and loud debates
(usually about cricket or politics) dominated life in this poor
man's Leaning Tower of Pisa. Partially hidden from view by
two large breadfruit and akee trees, the shabby three-room
wood structure leaned about two and a half degrees west,
looking none too regal on the green hillface. At first glance,
you would think a good high wind would topple it, but you'd
be mistaken. The Palace has withstood storms a plenty while
more imposing structures bit the dust. Was as if God,
Himself, was holding it up.

A few years back, the owner, Oscar 'Kofi' Blackman—a
bearded behemoth—announced that he dreamt he was
descendent of an African king and by virtue of this revelation

was appointing himself king of the village in preparation for the day when, according to this dream, a true true African woman would appear in the village to be his queen. By true true African, Kofi meant a woman born in Africa, since it was hard to even get most Bajans to accept they were of African descent. He quit his job as a well-digger and set about acquiring five more wives. That was how African kings lived, he claimed. Never mind he was already legally married to one of the nicest women in the village who'd borne two daughters in his corpulent image. She left him, taking the children, the minute she heard mention of other wives.

Kofi brought five women from neighboring villages, all in various stages of pregnancy, to live with him and flung the doors to his house wide open, decreeing that from that moment on it would be called: the Palace where all his subjects, high and low, would be welcome to air their complaints at any time. He instituted a series of taxes to support himself and his new family, promising in return to provide spiritual advice and illumination of life's mysteries to the residents of Chalky Mount since the churches were fooling people by promising them a place in a heaven which had room for one hundred and forty-four thousand people. All Israelites. As you might expect, nobody paid the taxes, but people took pity on the pregnant women and gave food. After two months, Kofi's wives got tired of going from house to house begging and deserted him.

Kofi's 'reign' came to a sorry end a few weeks later. One day he turned up at Geneva Samuel's door begging for corn-meal to make dumplings. Geneva, an inscrutable old woman living by herself on the edge of the village just where the white road disappeared into the darkness of the gully, called him a big tub of lard, and told him a man his size should have more respect for himself and that if she were his mother she would take a belt to his tail. From then nobody in the village would even give Kofi leftover dog food. Under threat of jail for not paying child support to his wife and the other five women, he was forced to resume his membership in the fraternity of well-diggers.

But the lasting legacy of Kofi's barefaced attempt to live off others was that the Palace remained open to any and everybody. All day long, men and women, young or old, employed or unemployed (mostly unemployed), attended Kofi's court where they found food, drink and laughter; a place to drown their sorrows, start a fleeting romance, or sever difficult relationships. It was the liveliest place in the village with the human traffic heaviest at midday and midnight.

The Palace welcomed all types: politicians, prostitutes, beggars, thieves, light-livers. Even somebody like me. Without fanfare, I, Percival Theodore Mansfield Springer, known throughout the island as Lady Simone, female impersonator extraordinaire, was brought to the Palace by Kofi himself, who'd seen my comedy routine and Nina Simone impersonation (my aunt said I favored her so you know what I look like) at a club in Nelson Street and invited me to perform at a fair in Chalky Mount. The crowd loved me, as always. And though I lived in Belleplaine at the time, about two miles away, I became a familiar face in the Palace and soon moved to Chalky Mount.

I had taken the name Lady Simone after an incident in high school. My mother left these sunny shores for England's frost when I was seven, leaving me in the care of an aunt who drank too much and changed boyfriends every time she got drunk. Whenever that happened she would dress me up in her clothes, makeup and all, and together we would dance and sing along with Nina Simone's records. One of her boyfriends gave me a guitar and taught me how to play, though it did not save him the next time my aunt got drunk.

After scoring the second highest marks nationwide in the 11-Plus exam, I began attending one of the most prestigious high school for boys in the island, but by the time I was thirteen I realized that dressing up in my aunt's clothes was more than a passing fancy. There was something different about me. I loved the feeling of being in woman's clothes. The makeup. The perfume. I loved pretending to be Nina Simone. When I reached fifteen I realized that, unlike most boys my age, I had not sprouted any kind of facial, underarm or pubic hair, my voice was not changing, and my muscles were underdeveloped. I spent more and more time dressing up as Nina Simone, trying to sing like her, trying to walk the way I imagined she walked, sitting the way I imagined she sat, smiling her wide handsome smile. I took my books to school in a handsome weave bag, which would've done Nina Simone proud. I was ridiculed for my so-called effeminate ways and was called names like Miss Springer and Lady Springer. One day I faced down a group of my teasers and said: If you want to call me anything, call me Lady Simone. Then I sashayed away leaving their mouths agape. That day, a star was born.

That was the high note of my secondary school life, which quickly began to unravel after that triumphant moment. A month later one of the boys who constantly tormented me, kissed me unexpectedly in the lavatory. Talk about being delirious. After that, I couldn't wait to be alone with him. But alas, one day we were caught kissing, hauled before the headmaster and summarily expelled.

My disastrous turn in life didn't stop there. Attempting to burn my schoolbooks in my aunt's backyard, I set her house on fire. The brightest boy in Buhbaydus, she used to brag about me before half her house went up in flames. After that, she just called me mad and had me locked up in Black Rock Mental Hospital for a year. I spent the time teaching the patients Latin. It was there that I blossomed fully into Lady Simone, playing guitar, singing songs and telling jokes to amuse the patients and to keep myself from going mad.

After my release, I sat my G.C.E's privately and passed all nine subjects. I wanted to become a teacher, but was turned down when my high school files were examined. I went back to being Lady Simone, which was infinitely more fun. Regaled as Lady Simone in tight-fitting silk dresses, I spent my nights in the city, performing at Club Orleans, a jazz club patronized by tourists, picking up stories and the occasional lover. It was there Kofi saw my act.

Wearing a bright yellow sea-island cotton shirt, white slacks, sandals and no makeup whatsoever (I only wore makeup at night or when I'm working), I was leaning against the stove in the kitchen doing my nails when Moses walked into the Palace. Two women were seated around the table: Solace, once considered the most beautiful women in the village and Carla, a buxom, petite beauty whose banana-thick lips made her the butt of jokes (told behind her back, for Carla carried a knife in her bosom, as did Solace). Carla was feeding us the details about the horn she just put on her wayward husband.

I love gossiping with my girlfriends but Moses was the sexiest man in Chalky Mount. Hell, on the island. The minute he walked into the Palace I bolted the kitchen for the main room.

The first time I saw Moses in the Palace I felt I would die if I didn't touch him. That day I made sure I found a way to brush against him before he left. The next week I moved to Chalky Mount, renting a little red house near the school. That was three years ago and since then I can't tell you all the fantasies I've had of Moses escaping from his drinking buddies to visit me in my red house, which may not look like much from the outside but inside it's fit for a Queen. I repainted all the walls white, replaced the half-rotted flooring with red hardwood, which I polish every week, and bought new furniture from Courts, including a king-size bed which practically took up the entire bedroom. I've got mirrors everywhere, and pictures of Nina Simone all over the house and when I heard that Moses loved Jackie Opel I went and got pictures of him too.

Afraid to pursue Moses openly I lived for his appearances in the Palace. I thought I'd found a perfect way to get closer to him without raising suspicion when he asked me to take notes at a meeting of the potters he'd called to discuss ways to get better prices for their wares from souvenir and gift shops. I took notes and typed them up professionally. Every one was impressed. That's when I decided to start the quarterly newsletter Going Pottery to profile different potters, down to their favorite jokes, food and music. Moses and a few other potters gave me money to have it photocopied and my friends helped me distribute it around Bridgetown, and at hotels and gift shops. I must've written something about Moses in every issue, making sure I interviewed him at length each time. I thought it was quite clever of me. Until I almost gave myself away with persistent questions about his love life.

"Why don't you have a girlfriend? You're a very good looking man."

He looked up from the roast breadfruit and flying fish he was eating inside his workshop. He swallowed and smiled. "You gine write that in the newsletter?"

"What?"

"That I'm a very good looking man."

"I don't know. You want me to?"

"No." He broke into the most provocative grin.

"But you ain't answer my question."

"I don't have an answer. I just don't."

His eyes drifted back to his plate of food.

"Ain't seen nobody you like?" I asked.

"I ain't looking."

"Maybe you looking for something different."

He looked up again, his eyes feverishly alive, searching my own.

"Like what?"

His tone punctured my courage and I couldn't tell him what I was thinking.

Not long after that he met this Iris. I haven't set eyes on her yet, and I don't even think I want to. From what I've heard, she was an American-born doctor who'd come to Barbados to research her Bajan roots. She met Moses at a gallery and fell in love on the spot with Moses and his work. I, for one, can certainly identify with that. The man is gorgeous. Slender, but not skinny, with the articulate bone structure of a Massai prince. And he was the most fearless and talented potter in

Chalky Mount. The latest gossip was that his American princess was looking to take Moses to the States. I am still kicking myself over that lost opportunity when I had a chance to declare my love.

Rum glass in hand, Kofi was sitting on a windowsill in the main room. Boat was reclining on the floor next to his sleeping dog, Bis-Bis, the meanest dog in the village. People said he was a devil dog. Only Boat could pet him. Boat claimed Bis-Bis could track duppies.

The other two people in the main room that day were Centipede, an old beggar passed out drunk on the floor and Pecong who ruled the floor, *pompousetting* about the recent death of a politician.

"I believe a woman poison him. I hear that from reliable sources. Everybody know he had nuff women. And I personally believe a jealous woman poison him."

When Moses entered the room, Kofi stood up to greet him. Kofi might've been the king of the Palace, but Moses ruled Chalky Mount.

"Ah Moses, boy, just the man I want to see. Where the hell you been? Seems like you been hiding from the boys, man. Is near a month now you ain't step foot in here. Come man, pour a drink and leh we talk. Been hearing nuff things 'bout you. See your name and picture big in the newspaper. You's a big shot and thing nowadays."

"After you," Moses replied puckishly. "Everybody know your glass empty, man. If my deaf grandmother was here she would hear the emptiness in that glass. Pour one if yuh drinking. You expect to trick big men all the time walking round with a big empty glass?"

Kofi picked up the rum bottle with a sheepish grin.

I leaned against the partition hoping Moses would say something to me. Anything. Even just hello.

"How you doing Simone?" he said.

I beamed. "Not bad. And you?"

"Tight. Things holding steady. You ain't drinking? Where you glass?"

"I on medication," I replied. "Can't drink for a couple of days."

He took the rum bottle from Kofi and poured a glass half full. "Who this Pecong talking 'bout that get poison?"

"Our dearly departed parliamentary representative. Filmore Steele ESQ. May his soul rest in peace," mocked Pecong.

"Yuh better don't let nobody hear you saying that," Moses cautioned. "Yuh could get lock up for saying them things."

"Lock up? For saying what I know is true? Is a new day, boy. New day. We independent now. Independent. You know what that mean? We ain't beholden to nobody. No more masters. No more foreigners ruling we. Telling we what to do. I could cuss that white woman sitting pon that throne in England and nobody can't touch me." Pecong sucked his teeth loudly, poured a drink and swallowed hard. "And I glad we got we own money, so I don't have to see she dry ass face on we money no more neither."

Kofi incited. "So tell we more 'bout Filmore, man."

Pecong picked up the cue. "I, myself, sleep with one of his outside women. Nearly break she in two with the bamboo. She was so happy to get a real man she tell me all she secrets. Tell me he used to beat she up. If he wasn't such a old man I woulda put some licks in he rass meself, but I don't like unfairing old people."

In the kitchen my girlfriends heard this and brought their conversation to a halt. Pecong was forever talking about sharing licks. At least one of them had confided to me that the only licks Pecong ever shared were with his face glued between her legs, and he was piss-poor at that. They came into the main room, taking seats on the floor to hear the rest of the conversation.

"I don't use my tongue unless I got something important to say. You know that, Moses," Pecong continued.

"That ain't what I hear," Solace said with a laugh. The other two women chuckled.

"Who talking to you?"

"We want to know who give you this information," Boat said.

"Man, you think I so foolish? You expect me to give names with these lick-mouth women in here, especially that Lady Simone. A fly can't shite without she broadcasting it. Next thing you know, she on stage telling the world I say Filmore get poison. How long you think it going take for me name to get back to Filmore family? Not that I frighten for he family. I will give you all the names you want when these women gone."

"Listen fellas," Moses interjected. "I come here too tell you all something. Something very important."

"Man you ain't see I got the floor?" Pecong whined, his face suddenly tightening.

Moses, like everyone else, saw the change in his friend's demeanor. "You got the floor? Then keep it. I ain't want the floor. I just want to say a few words to my friends. As most of you know by now, my three big Monkeys win first prize in the National Independence Arts Competition. Well, what I here to tell you is that soon them going to be in the museum for the whole entire island to see. And they may even get put on display in New York. Wunna know what that means? I got a letter from the Prime Minister himself that say so. He want me to come down and see him."

"Yuh making sport, man," Kofi said gleefully, slapping Moses so hard on the back the slender man fell to the floor.

"Sorry, man." Kofi helped Moses to his feet. "You telling me you going to meet with our Maximum Leader and that them going to put your Monkeys in the museum? Man, I didn't even know we had a museum in this country. What so them got in it? Anything from Barbados, or all the stuff come from Away like everything else in this country? Man, this is great news. I think. We will have to go to this museum now, won't we boys?"

I wanted to go over and hug Moses but I knew that would've been too fresh.

"I can't wait to see these Monkeys in the museum, Moses." Carla said, caressing Moses' elbow.

Dressed in his customary all-black with shirt buttoned down, Boat got up from the floor to shake Moses' hand.

"Yes, man, I proud of you," Boat said. "You do a lot for this village and now you doing more. You was the first to realize how much the tourist shops and galleries was ripping off the potters, buying their things for next to nothing and turning round and selling them to tourists at high prices. And if you didn't organize the potters to speak up, the tourist shops and galleries woulda never give them a fair dollar. I have to admire what you doing. You showing how the Small Man just as important as the Big Man."

" How you figure that, Boat? What does putting Monkeys in the museum got to do with small man or big man or any of that shite?" Pecong said, disdainfully. "And any of wunna see what Moses got paint on these Monkeys?"

Kofi said, "Wuh wrong with them."

Boat scratched his scraggly beard thoughtfully. "I studied them careful. Ain't nothing wrong with what he got paint. What wrong with a woman giving birth? A woman had to give birth for each one of we to be here. Ain't that right, Centipede?"

Boat kicked Centiped in the ribs to wake him up.

Centipede wriggled and grunted without opening his eyes. "Gimme the glass leh me fire one, man."

Everybody laughed.

Pecong tried another tack. "Wunna think now that Moses screwing this American woman and winning big prize he going to care 'bout you all up here?"

"Yes Moses, man." Kofi poured a drink and moved to stand in the open doorway. He threw back his head and tipped the glass, squeezing his eyes shut and swallowed. "I didn't want to bring it up, but we been hearing these rumors 'bout you and this doctor woman. I ain't see it but everybody else say them see she big Jaguar park off side the road by your house. How come you ain't bring she in the Palace to meet the boys?"

Moses sighed wearily and poured a rum with a forced smile. He gulped the liquor and set the glass upside-down beside the bottle to thwart the buzzing flies. "Man, you all listening to me or not? I talking 'bout something big. Soon you going see all kinds of people coming up here. From all over. Reporters. Tourists. Art collectors. This going to help everybody. Don't listen to Pecong. He is me friend, but you all know how Pecong can get when he jealous. I doing something that could radically change the way people in this country look at we. Maybe even the way the country think 'bout itself."

"But we still want to know if you going to the States," Kofi said.

Pecong snapped. "Man, if he want to go to the States leh he go long and carry long them scandalous, obscene things he call art."

"Do you know what the births symbolize?" Moses asked.

"Symbolize shite. I don't care what them symbolize. How many Bajans you think going to care about what them births symbolize?"

"The births represent the transitions of Barbados. The birth on the first Monkey represent the birth of the first Bajan born on the island into slavery. The second birth is the birth of the first Bajan born into freedom after slavery get abolish. And the last one is the first Bajan born after we get independence. The three births…"

Pecong interrupted him. "Man I couldn't care less if it was ten births. You got a painting of a woman with she thing splatter open and a baby dripping blood coming out, talking 'bout that is art. That ain't art. That is nastiness. And mark my word, when the religious people see them it going be real strife in this country. The judges at the Arts Festival musta been drunk when they give you that prize. Man, I don't know how you could call that shite art. And don't pretend you doing this for the people up here. You doing this to impress them artsy-farsty people who own galleries. And that half-white woman that looking to take you back to America with she. As for being jealous. Why should I be jealous of you? I had women all 'bout this Buhbayduss. All kinds of women. Women that wouldn't look twice at your skinny rass. You think I care 'bout your pawpaw color foreigner?"

I'd heard enough. I stepped to the center of the room, looked around slowly with a smile that made my rockstone cheeks arch majestically. "Yuh know Pecong, sometimes you does get on so silly it does make me want to puke," I began. "Here it is, Moses come in here to show you how one man with vision, with ideas, with dreams could influence powerful people and change this country, and you more interested in pissing yourself over nonsense than what Moses got to say. And you say you is he best friend. Man, sometimes I think you does forget you brain under the bed."

"Look, Simone." Pecong poked me hard in my chest, "You better sit down and shut your bulling she-she rass before we stop you from coming in the Palace. We tired hearing your blasted stale ass jokes anyway."

Kofi stepped between us and pushed Pecong away. Pecong was well-built but Kofi outweighed him by about one hundred pounds.

"Man, how many times I have to tell you to stop talking to Simone like that? I bet you can't even spell the word she-she." He looking Pecong directly in the eyes. "I don't care what you say about Simone outside, but in here you treat her with respect. You don't call her no buller nor no she-she. You got that? Or me and you going to tumble. We like she just the way she is. She belong in the Palace just like you or anybody else. In fact, I would put you out before I put she out. When your rass wanted somebody to write that application letter for that job at Palm Tree Hotel who you ask? Simone. Why? Cause she happen to be the only body in here who ain't get their education at the pipe."

Nervous laughter filled the room.

"I, for one, getting a little tired of she coming in here talking to me like I still in primary school," Pecong countered. "I don't care how much certificates she got. Them certificates ain't worth the paper she does use to wipe she rass. She still can't get a decent job."

"I got a job," I said.

"What? Pretending you's some drug addict American singer?"

"Nina Simone is not a drug addict," I corrected.

They're all drug addicts," Pecong charged. "All them blasted American singers are drug addicts."

"So tell we Moses." Kofi turned away, cutting the argument short, "We know you's a man ain't seen a tie that don't remind you of a belt. When you go to see the PM you going to wear a tie?"

Everybody started laughing again. Except Pecong.

Pecong and Moses grew up next door to one another. They were about the same age, and have been best friends for the longest time. Rumor was ripe that they had a falling out over this same American woman, Iris. Apparently, she came to visit Moses one day when he was out. Pecong happened to be at Moses' house that day. Truth was, Pecong always at somebody else's house, because he didn't have a house of his own, and he couldn't live with his mother because he and she had a falling out over her new boyfriend. But I straying off the point. Pecong couldn't resist trying to get Iris in bed, because that is just the way Pecong is. We called him the crotchhound.

Even though the American woman made it clear that Moses was the only man she was interested in Pecong wouldn't take no for an answer and tried to kiss the woman. I could see Pecong doing that. And, well, she slapped him and left.

Solace stood up, poured a drink, downed it quickly, then lit a cigarette. In her youth, Solace was one of those pretty-skin women that drove Bajan men crazy, but she'd seen better days. She had lost some of her teeth and the alcohol had her face wrung to a side, like a beat up fender. Eyes baleful as ever, she closing in on Moses behind a wedge of smoke. When the smoke cleared she was close enough to kiss him.

"Why you's a good one though, Moses. Every time I talk to you, yuh tell me you ain't looking for no woman and now I hear you got a 'merican woman?" She thumped her chest around her heart. "Yuh know I been holding this thing in me chest for you for the longest time, too."

"Yuh better make sure it ain't a cold," Boat quipped.

Moses knew better than to answer Solace. The glaze of intoxication had already devoured her face. In this half-drunk state, with her tiny black eyes half-shut, she was liable to do and say anything. Many men had taken advantage of Solace in this state. A long time ago, Moses found himself in bed with her in the Palace bedroom, but they were both too drunk to screw. For that reason, it seemed, Solace was always offering herself to him.

"You need to get yuhself a man, Solace," Pecong said.

"Guess that rules you out, 'cause you barely got enough in your pants to qualify as a boy."

The room romped with laughter.

"You let she talk to you like that, man?" cackled Boat.

"I don't pay she no mind," muttered Pecong, "I tired skinning she up all 'bout the bush."

"You ain't know who want skinning up? Yuh old worthless mother."

Pecong sprang to the center of the room a few feet from where Solace was slinging her godhorse frame around Moses. She spun to face him, knife in hand, eyes fixed, showing no fear. Moses jumped between the two combatants. Putting his arm around Solace, he led her off to the other end of the room.

Pecong screamed at her back, "Yuh betta stop walkin' 'bout giving people the clap, yuh nasty whore!"

Solace turned sharply around, eager to return to the fray but Moses held her firm. Gradually she relaxed, allowing herself to be comforted by him, liking it more and more each second. Moses released his hold. She continued to lean on him.

"Solace, you know better than to talk 'bout Pecong mother. You know how sensitive he is on that subject."

Moses tried to move away, but Solace reached out and held his hand intently.

She whispering the way drunks whisper, loud enough for the whole world to hear. "You got any money, Moses? I need to borrow twenty dollars."

"What for?"

"I have to go to the doctor tomorrow."

"What's wrong?"

"I don't know. Been having some shooting pains in me side of late."

Moses' eyes followed hers to the ground. Cracks were beginning to appear between the floorboards where the linoleum had been ripped away. Bits of food, cigarette butts and mango skins glossed with dirt made a shiny mosaic on the floor.

When Solace looked up her eyes were wet.

Moses couldn't have been fooled by Solace's watery eyes; like most of us, he knew all of Solace's tricks.

Solace said, "I ask you 'cause I know you would give it to me if you had it. And look, I ain't asking you to give me for nothing, yuh know. Like, maybe tonight I could come by your place or we could meet somewhere and I could give you something in return."

"Something like what?"

"Anything you want. Anything at all. You know anything I got is yours."

Moses reached into his pocket, pulled out two bills, a twenty and a five; he gave her the twenty. She smiled as the money disappeared into her bosom.

A look of brotherly concern came over Moses' face. "Yuh know, you should stop knocking 'bout the place and find something to do."

"What I going find to do now, Moses? Who going give me a job?" She paused. "Should I come by tonight?"

He shook his head.

She turned and went out the side door, her cat-steps soundless on the linoleum.

"Man, I can't believe you give her money," Pecong pounced.

"Why you don't mind yuh own blasted business?"

"Why you always sticking up for that whore?"

"Maybe you should just leave her alone."

"Leave her lone? What I do she? She always borrowing money from you and never pay back a red cent. And what you does get for it? Nothing. That's why women would always take advantage of you, man. Yuh trust them too much. Man, I bet she going down the road laughing at you. And she go probably buy some man a bottle of rum, get drunk and get screw, and tomorrow she going to be broke and begging for money again."

Moses remained silent.

"He right, yuh know, Moses," Kofi said.

"So what, man? What's the big effin deal? Sometimes I does come here and spend a hundred dollars on rum and food, and I don't hear nobody complaining. So what if she take the money and spend it on a man? I don't care, yuh understand? I give her the money, she can do whatever she want with it." Moses turned around in a circle like one of those Chinese martial arts heroes defending an assault from all sides. "Maybe if you all had something better to do than sit around here drinking rum and talking shite, you won't worry so much 'bout what Solace do and don't do. How much longer wunna plan to live like this? Independence don't only mean we getting the Queen off we money, yuh know. It also mean we going to have to work harder to make this country something and stop trying to live off of other people."

"See that. See that, fellas?" Pecong said provocatively. "You all hear that? What I tell you? All of a sudden Moses believe he's more than we 'cause he smelling up under that 'merican woman armpit."

"Man, I can't believe you getting on so childish. I thought you was me friend. Because Iris laugh in you face this is the way you treat me? What you want from me, man? You want me to beg Iris to give you a little piece? You waan know how it feel to screw an American woman?"

"I don't need no 'merican woman. She ain't nothing special. You think she really want your uneducated rass? How long you thing you going to be able to keep she? Man, you so foolish. She going to use you up and then throw you way like a dirty Modess."

This brought guffaws from Kofi and Boat.

I knew it the moment his eyes fell on my face that Moses was done with the Palace. Forever. He'd outgrown this house which had become our place of worship. Everyone else must've sensed it. My heart sank. This was the last time we would see Moses in the Palace.

He stepped around Centipede on the floor, clipping his heel against the short man's shoulder.

Kofi's voice pursued him. "Where you going, man? You coming back? Moses!"

Moses was already striding across the tired grass at the front yard.

If Moses wasn't coming back to the Palace there was no reason for me to be there. I wanted to follow him out that door. But the truth is, I didn't have the courage.

SLY MONGOOSE

"that will be eighty dollars, miss."

Esther turned and stared blankly at the taxi driver's dark sweating face. She had not heard a single word. Since they left the airport, on the southern tip of the island, her mind had been completely focused on one thing: would she be able to go through with her plan; and if so, what would she do when she saw him.

"I'm sorry," she said meekly.

"Eighty dollars Barbados. Or forty U.S."

She looked outside at the house perched on the rise. Her mother's house. The house where Esther grew up. A place of many wonderful memories: waking up to the smell of coconut bread baking; the sound of rain drumming on the windows in the middle of the night; hiding under a chair in the kitchen listening to her aunts talk about sex.

For all that, this would be the first time Esther would be staying here on any of her trips back to the island. All her previous visits found her staying in hotels. Her choice. And, one that caused her mother no end of grief. How strange will it be staying here now her mother was dead?

She opened her purse and took out fifty US dollars. "Keep the change."

His whole face expanded when he smiled. "Thank you. Not to be rude, but can I ask you a question?"

The driver's halting voice reminded her how smoothly the bajan accent melts into your senses once you have hot sun to go with it.

"What is it?"

He got out and opened her door. "Is everything alright? You seem a little sad."

"I'm fine, but thanks."

"You live here or in Away?"

"I live in Philadelphia."

"Long time?"

"Twenty years."

"Well, no matter how long you gone, be it one year or a hundred, the rock is always home."

She smiled and stepped onto the rutted asphalt and felt the rushing sun warm the back of her neck. Hot day, but windy too. Standing at the edge of the road, she watched him remove her bags from the trunk. A stiff wind tousled the arched green tips of coconut trees in the valley below. Above them, delicious untarnished white clouds danced along with brio.

Gripping the heavy Samsonite suitcase by its silver handle, the driver lifted it as easily as if it was a bucket of water. With her brown leather bag in the other hand, he marched up the steps to the front door and set them down in the verandah.

"Thank you," She said.

"You're quite welcome. It's always nice to welcome Bajans back to the rock. You here for Crop-Over?"

"No, actually."

"Oh, It going be hot this year."

"Oh, my! Really? Hotter than usual?"

He laughed. "I was talking about the music not the weather."

She knew very little about Crop-Over. The festival was started after she'd left the island in 1974. She had never attended because it took place in July and August, the hottest months of the year. After so many years in North America excessive heat made her dizzy.

"Nuff things for the calypsonians to sing 'bout," the driver continued. "This place going off-track. I don't know what going become of this little rock if we continue the way we going. If you get a chance you should go to a tent. Hear what the calypsonians singing 'bout."

"I'll see. Thanks again."

He handed her a card. "Name's Mort. If you need somebody to drive you around, gimme a call. If you don't like calypso, there's always Lady Simone. He performs at club Orleans on weekends. Big show. Everybody loves him. He sweet fuh days. Funny as ram-goat. And he really sound just like Nina Simone fuh truth. I can pick you up if you want."

Esther took the card, "You said Lady Simone, but then you said he."

The driver flashed his rubbery smile. "When you see him you will understand."

She was still puzzled but the driver had turned and was descending the steps back to his car. He got in and the vehicle moved off slowly. When it had disappeared over the ridge she turned and opened her bag to search for the key.

she expected it to be musty inside, but wasn't prepared for the stench which greeted her. No one had lived here since her mother got admitted to the Queen Elizabeth hospital two months ago, and clearly her brother, Kevin, who still lived on the island, had not been around to air it out either.

Esther waited at the threshold for her senses to adapt to the onslaught of fetid odors. In the fusty quiet she heard her mother's distressed voice. The reaction was always the same whenever Esther arrived with the news that she would be staying at a hotel once again.

"But how you could you do that to me?"

"What am I doing to you, Mummy? It's better this way."

"Don't talk rubbish, Esther. How can staying at a hotel be better than staying here? I just don't understand you. How can you come back here and stay in a hotel? Eating that expensive, bad-tasting food."

"I can afford it, Mummy."

"You know what my friends saying?"

"I don't care what your friends are saying. It's my life. My money. I can afford it. Leave me alone. Would you rather I not come back?"

That was how her visits usually began. And ended. With the two of them fighting over her decision to stay in a hotel.

There would be no such admonishments from her mother this time. Last week she succumbed to the cancer which had only been diagnosed six months ago.

Esther dragged the suitcases inside then opened all the windows downstairs to let in fresh air. Almost immediately, the green gauze-thin curtains flapped in the wind. She took off her shirt and began to unhook her pushup bra. A memory unfurled before her and she stopped midway.

It had started with him peeping through her bedroom window as she got dressed. After that came the sweet talk. She turned heels on the memory and continued undressing. After releasing her breasts, she unzipped her hip-hugging skirt, letting it fall to the ground. Now, all that was left was the black thong. That came off, too. As she bent to pick up thong and skirt, she reflected on how many years it'd taken her to get the confidence to wear anything this provocative. She folded the skirt neatly over the back of the divan then went to open the windows upstairs.

She found one upstairs room locked. Deciding to deal with that puzzle later, she went back downstairs to the kitchen. Looking out through the kitchen window she again allowed herself to be caught up in the reverie of her mother's voice. Sunday morning, singing as she seasoned chicken or pork for lunch.

Rock of Ages
Cleft for Me,
Let me hide myself in thee

"Esther, girl, why you don't come inside and put something on your feet? You don't see how dirty it is out there?

You so hard-ears. Look at your feet. Hard and flat like a man. You's a young lady, don't you know that? Your feet shouldn't look like you went digging cane holes."

That lecture she heard on a daily basis. Esther hated wearing shoes when she was small, preferring the visceral connection of her skin on the ground or grass; even after she busted her big toe on a rock one time, and was bitten by a centipede another.

The yard was now so cluttered that a mouse would have a hard time finding a place to hide. Her mother had trouble getting rid of stuff. Crammed into what was once a spacious yard were several generations of broken-down furniture, cases on cases of empty soda bottles, three old fridges, broken cement blocks and other detritus from the reconstruction of the house. Esther recognized the boxy wrought iron set which crammed their living room when she was a child.

She heartened at the susurrus of curtains behind her ruffled by a gust off the sea. A most Barbadian sound. The sound of her youth.

But more than any thing, the sound of her youth was the sound of her mother singing. No one had a voice like her mother. Esther was convinced that had her mother been born in America she would've found fame as a gospel singer. The clarity and brightness of her mother's soprano was still palpable.

To this day, Esther still woke up on Sunday mornings in her Philadelphia brownstone across from the park thinking she heard her mother singing. It was a shame that she'd cut herself off from that pleasure for so long; now she would never hear it again.

She fought the tears welling in her eyes and turned to open the fridge. Fumes of decay smacked her in the face. She reeled, then took a deep breath. First order of business would be to restore sanity to the fridge. She stuck her head back inside to assess the task before her. Wasn't as bad as it smelled. A soggy half-eaten chocolate cake. Shriveled tomatoes. A cracked block of moldy cheese. Withered cabbage salad in a glass bowl. Aha! The culprit!

After cleaning the fridge she would pick out the clothes to bury her mother, who'd left specific instructions on her burial garments. In a few days, she would go with Kevin to the funeral home to dress her mother. She was nervous about that. But her mother had also left strict orders that her children, and only her children, should dress her body.

She looked forward to spending time with Kevin every time she came home. This time, he will be added comfort for her. He would've met her at the airport had he not been called away to an emergency business meeting in St. Lucia where he co-owned a hotel.

Her brother was gay. After her mother found out about his lifestyle things were never the same between them. Kevin had always been her mother's favorite and the news simply devastated her. Esther understood why, but that didn't make her anymore sympathetic to her mother's stance.

Everytime Esther came to visit she had to listen to her mother's lament about the prospects of not getting any grandchildren: "You can't stay married, and Kevin don't like woman. Why you all punishing me like this?"

Kevin had recently started seeing someone new and Esther expected she would get a chance to meet him before her trip was over, though Kevin had seemed unaccustomedly coy about revealing his new lover's identity.

Growing up, it seemed to her that Kevin was being groomed to replace her father. Or to be the man her father failed to become in her mother's eyes. Her mother spent so much time bragging to friends about how bright Kevin was—no matter that Esther was the smarter of the two—that Esther was very happy to get off the island to study abroad, fully expecting that Kevin would've stayed behind. But when he finished high school he, too, went overseas to study.

Esther took a shower in the upstairs bathroom. From there, she could see into the yard of the house next door, which had changed owners over the years, but still looked much the same as she remembered it growing up. Back then, the modest wood house was owned by a man who tutored both her and Kevin. Over the years, most home owners in the village had converted their houses from wood to brick, and had added on at least a bedroom or two. Many of the more image-conscious homeowners, like her mother, had completely redone their homes to reflect a growing trend for two-story houses sweeping the island.

In the process of lathering her thighs, she glanced up and saw something, which gave her a shiver; a vision that often repulsed her when she was a little girl. The sight of the long furry creature skulking through the grass just beyond the fenced-in yard of the house next door squeezed from her throat a tiny gasp of fear for the frisky baby chicks in the yard. She wanted to scream a warning, but knew it would be pointless. Where was the mother hen?

The mongoose wormed through a hole in the fence, moving with calculated precision, as if it knew exactly which of the chicks would be his dinner. A loud cackle erupted from an area behind a large water tank. The mother hen had discovered the danger. With wings flapping helplessly, she came rushing toward her fuzzy-haired offspring. Alas! She was too late. The mongoose had already snatched one yellow chick, which had not even uttered a sound, and had slithered back through the hole in the fence, disappearing like a ghost into the march of grass.

she unlocked the door with a key found in her mother's bedroom. On one of Esther's visits to the hospital a month ago, her mother had given her the combination to the bedroom safe. There, her mother told her, all the papers for the house, and information about her financial assets would be found. The key was lodged between the pages of Proverbs in a leather-bound bible sitting on the top shelf of the safe. Esther remembered buying the bible in London as as a birthday present for her mother.

As she picked up the key a yellow-highlighted passage at the bottom of the page caught her eye.

Stolen waters are sweet, and bread eaten in secret is pleasant. But he knoweth not that the dead are there; and that her guests are in the depths of hell.

She stood in the doorway listening to the lifelessness. The air was dank and still. She thought of cracking a window to let in air and light but decided against it. No need. Nothing but a storage room. Empty barrels stacked one on top of the other. A bed stood upright against a wall. Looked like the one she had in her bedroom when she was young. A small mahogany dresser in a corner was still in good shape. Esther remembered that, too. Definitely came from her bedroom. Still had the scratches she made with a small knife, for which she got a good lashing. Her mother used to say that things made of mahogany lasted forever. Too bad souls aren't made of mahogany.

Perhaps Esther shouldn't have been surprised to see so many of her old school books piled neatly against a wall. These books were the bricks of her mother's untamed pride in giving Esther the education she never had. There was no way her mother would've gotten rid of these books. Another reverie. Her mother sipping tea by the lowside window taking credit for Esther's success.

"If I didn't sent you to lessons, you wouldn't have passed for Foundation."

But perhaps she learned her lessons too well. For now she was alone. Afraid to trust men. The three men she married and divorced all loved her. They said they did. She enjoyed sex with them (though she never achieved an orgasm with either one). Greg, the Jewish tennis pro who spoke fluent French and taught her how to control the two-handed backhand, she loved him, perhaps more than any man. But it always seemed like he wanted more of something she could not find to give him. She wasn't uptight in bed. They went out often, and also enjoyed intimate dinners at home together. They took long walks along Penn's Landing. She laughed at his jokes (and he wasn't very funny). Yet, it wasn't enough. He couldn't touch her, he said.

She opened one of the books: *A Short History of the West Indies*, by Philip Sherlock. A cloud of dust rose off the page. There was her name, scrawled across the first page in black ink. One thing was clear. Her handwriting hadn't changed much.

She spied the dust-grayed copy of *Tropic of Cancer* wedged between *The Prince* and her favorite book of all time: *Jane*

Eyre. She wavered between Bronte and Miller for a second before settling on *Tropic of Cancer*. She brushed the thick film of dust from the cover and opened to the first chapter.

He had given her that book. One of the most important novels ever written. That was his claim. And she had believed him. She was thirteen. He was her tutor, one of the most learned men in the village. Why shouldn't she have believed him?

She was suddenly flushed with shame at the memory of nights spent devouring those pages. Every strange, startling, explicit word. Why did she enjoy reading it so much? Surely, not because it was one of the most important books ever written. She wasn't even sure she understood what that meant at the time, or for that matter, what it would mean now if someone were to say that to her. What makes a novel important?

She acknowledged, however, that when he vouchsafed this book it gave her the liberty to read and absorb its lustiness without skepticism. But it also opened the way for much more. Days and nights she wished she could reclaim.

the next day she found him in the telephone directory, the third entry under Bishop. That surprised her. She expected it would've been more difficult to locate him. He was now a big-shot in the country. A member of parliament no less. Those kinds of people were usually harder to find, except at election time, of course.

To keep the element of surprise on her side, she decided not to call. Instead, she contacted Mort, the taxi driver. He came in half an hour, his smile as supple as ever.

"I was just having a beer with my friends," he offered. "But when I hear it was you I tell them I had work to do."

When she gave him the address, Mort said he knew the house well. It was in a secluded area near the beach in St. John. He'd driven there many times. A very important man, Mort stressed. But secretive, too, even though he was a public figure.

"What do you mean by secretive," she asked him.

"He don't be out much in public. He does keep to himself."

"How did he get elected to public office if he's so private?"

"You know how Barbados is, too," he replied

"What do you mean?"

"Don't get on like you don't know what I mean."

She didn't want to laugh, but she was amused. "I really don't."

"He got one of the sweetest mouths in the country. And we like sweet-mout' politicians. He could tantalize you with the words. Don't get me wrong, everybody say he's one of the smartest people on the island. He know a lot about tourism and stuff like that. Before he get into politics he used run a small airline somewhere in South America."

"Oh, he was off the island?"

"Yeah, he only come back 'bout here roughly ten years ago. People does flock to hear him speak on the platform. He does turn a phrase better than my grandmother does turn coucou. And since he become a minister he do a lot for old people and he help out artists that suffering. Especially the old-time calypsonians. Help them get housing and stuff like that. I don't like he, but he sweet."

"Why don't you like him?"

"Is he a friend of yours?" Mort stole a glance into the back-seat, before quickly returning his focus on the road.

She hesitated. "No."

"He too nasty fuh me."

"Nasty?"

"The rumors flying 'bout here like sandflies."

"What kind of rumors?"

"He does give a lot of parties."

"Is that something he shouldn't be doing?"

"Is the kind of people who does go to these parties."

"What kind of people?"

"It ain't fuh people... people that... You know this is a funny country."

"How so?"

"You can't always talk over what you hear. This is a place where you does see things and does got to pretend you ain't seen nothing. You know what I mean? This man does got parties and you couldn't find one woman inside the place. Not one woman. I does drive people there. People does come from all over the world to go to his parties. Important people from Jamaica and Norway and America. Not one women."

"And that's wrong?"

"If it wrong? You think it right?"

"I'm asking you."

He laughed from his belly. "You see what I mean. You's a real Bajan, though."

he said he wasn't surprised to see her.

"I'm sorry about your mother. She was a fine woman."

"I read that you're now an evolved minister in the government. Helping destitute artists."

He walked around to the back of her chair. Oddly, she wasn't afraid being alone with him.

"You've been reading up on me?"

"I read a lot."

He touched her hair. Without looking around, she brushed his hand away.

"It's a rewarding job. Difficult at times. Exasperating most of the times. But I can bring about a lot of change in this country."

"Still looking to change lives?"

"It's rewarding to change people's lives."

"Is that how you feel about changing mine?"

"I understand you're a doctor, and you have a good practice in the States."

"Who told you that?"

"Your mother."

"You spoke to my mother about me?"

"She lived in my constituency. I try to stay close to my constituents. Every time I go back to the old neighborhood I go to look her up."

"She never mentioned that to me."

"Perhaps she forgot."

"Perhaps she knew it would upset me," said Esther. "I'm beginning to wonder if she knew."

"If she knew what?"

"If she knew what you were doing to me."

He didn't speak for a while. She could sense his prodigious intellect at work. How long would it take him to establish why she was there.

He slipped across the bright wood floor to a rack of CDs in a stainless steel tower. "Would you like to hear some music? You used to love Beethoven, if I remember correctly."

"Your memory is failing you."

"I doubt that. I made sure you listened to a piece of Beethoven before and after every lesson."

I haven't listened to him in years. Not since I left the island."

"Is that so? That's quite a shame. Quite a loss, I should say."

"A loss?"

"Yes. It was so much a part of your development."

"I prefer Gabby."

He laughed. "I know you're joking, but that's okay. He's a fine composer in his own way."

"More relevant than Beethoven. Do you ever listen to him?"

"Yes, of course. I fully immerse myself in the culture of Barbados. I listen to the music. I go to the plays, what few they are. I visit the museum and art shows. Lots of talent there. I try to live as intensely in the present as I possibly can."

"But do you really listen to Gabby's music?"

"Yes, and your suggestion that he's better than Beethoven is ridiculous and you know it. But that's just like you. Provocative to the point of being ridiculous."

"I didn't say better. More relevant to our place and time. Appropriate."

"Appropriate? Are we talking about the weather or art?"

"Gabby speaks in a musical vernacular that's understood by everybody in this country. He's appropriate for Barbados."

"That's nonsense. And you are fully aware of that. I don't agree with that at all. That's like saying my grandmother's bush-medicine is more appropriate for our medical needs than someone like you."

"How do you know that isn't true?"

"Because genius... real art transcends the parochial. Borders cannot confine it. It speaks to our common need to understand why we are here. Just like true science tries to solve the common problem of living better and more comfortable lives."

She wanted to laugh. He may've gotten older but one thing about him hadn't changed. By the inflection of his voice, he still betrayed his impatience with an argument he considered silly or jejune. However, she wasn't cowed by his mannerisms anymore.

"You speak as if your grandmother's goal wasn't as lofty."

"Perhaps they were. Though I doubt it. The difference is that she had no way of affecting anybody's life other than mine. And those immediately accessible to her."

"You force fed Beethoven down my throat but I can't say any of it stuck."

"It changed you in ways that you probably don't know. It opened you up."

"Was that your goal? To open me up? For what?"

He took a CD from the rack. "I'm proud of the work I did with you and your brother. And I'm also proud to say that I have Gabby's latest compilation here. Nothing new. But a lot of his better stuff. You want to listen?"

"No. I can listen to it at home."

He fiddled with the CD in his hand. "I'm curious. Why did you put it that way?"

"Why did I put it that way? Are you for real?"

"It wasn't like that."

"Like how?

"It wasn't like I raped you. It wasn't like that."

"Wasn't it?"

"No."

"That's exactly what it was. Look up the statute. Do you know what you did to me?"

"You wanted it, Esther."

"How can you say that? You don't know what I wanted. You had no interest in what I wanted."

"The way you acted. The way... The way you... You enjoyed it." He paused, thinking. "You came back. You came time and time again."

"I was a child. Children always come back for candy."

"You were very mature."

"Listen to yourself. And you call yourself educated?"

"You came back," he said again, as if he hadn't heard her.

"I came back. Is that the only thing you have to say? Do you know why I came back?"

He paused. "Because you wanted more."

She thought about his response. Because she wanted more. But more of what? It was the question she'd been trying to answer for years. In therapy. During sleepless nights. Driving home from work. At the end of each unsatisfactory relationship. But no matter how many times she waded through the quagmire of those three years she found nothing to grasp. Nothing to explain why she couldn't move beyond the shame.

The question suffused her world with guilt. Why did she go back time after time? He was right. She wanted more. She had never admitted that to herself. She had never admitted it to the therapist and perhaps that was why therapy had failed so miserably.

Yes, she wanted more. But more of what? She did not go back because she wanted more sex. That much she was clear on. Otherwise the deep feelings of guilt, and the insecurity which has dogged her ever since, would not have lingered for so long.

She remembered the argot of his seduction. It was music to her ears at the time.

You're the most beautiful creature in the world.

It didn't sound corny then.

You're my darling.

Nobody had ever called her 'darling' before. Not like that. And not since.

Your diamond is yet to shine.

He was prophetic on that one.

No one will ever love you like me.

Arrhhh fuck!

her father could do anything with his hands, her mother used to say. He built the simple chattel house they lived in. It took him five years, building one room at a time, but he finished it all by himself. Then he died.

Esther was six when it happened. She remembered he was tall and brown-skinned. He drove a truck for a construction company which paid decent money. One rainy day the truck ran off the road and flipped. She remembered that day. She remembered the rain. She remembered going to see him in the hospital before he died. She hated rainy days after that.

Their living room looked out onto a hill dappled with cherry and guava trees. In the evening, when the bucolic life in her hardscrabble village was its most poignant, she would pick fruit and play with her friends in the grass on the hill. She enjoyed playing *Simon Says*, but *Brown Girl in the Ring* was her favorite game. Always the brownest girl in the ring, she relished the opportunity to dance and show off during the 'show me your motion' part of the game. But those sweet memories of her youth were often trapped and enslaved by terrifying dreams that had been slowly incubating in her mind over the years.

Bishop lived alone next door to them and was respected throughout the village for his brightness. That's the one thing people always said about him. *He bright as shite.* Esther heard it roll off the tongues of old drunken men in the rum shops, and dropped, without falter, from the lips of old woman walking along the cart-roads. She heard in spill from her mother's mouth in the morning and at night when she prayed that her children would grow up to be as learned as her neighbor.

She was thirteen when she first realized she had a crush on him. The notion of his age-superiority could not sway her galloping heart. Then again, she could not have known that he was at least 20 years older.

Esther's mother had asked him to tutor Esther and Kevin. He agreed. They went to his house three times a week for lessons in Mathematics and English. But he also introduced them to music and art. Each lesson began and finished with him playing a piece of classical music on his piano.

One evening, just before dusk, she was in her bedroom getting dressed to go to his house for a lesson. She'd just taken a bath. She always powdered her body after a bath, the way her mother taught her. Helped to beat back the tropical heat. She powdered her underarms and her back, and was about to powder between her legs.

When she looked up he was standing at her bedroom window. She always kept her windows open because the flowered curtains were opaque. He'd moved the curtains aside and was looking at her naked body. She was trapped for a long time in that moment. For years, in fact. She never understood what it meant. She knew what it did. Opened up a path for him which she didn't know how to close.

"I was coming to tell you and your brother that I have to go out. Lessons canceled for this evening."

"can i have some water?"

"I'm expecting someone. You should go."

"Not until I get what I came here for?"

"What did you come here for? An apology?"

"Can I have some water, please?"

He left her sitting on the white sofa next to the baby grand in the large square room. The epitome of rationality and order. Paintings of faces and bodies equidistant from each other on the milk-white walls.

She did not win an island scholarship as he had predicted, but she came damn close. She got an exhibition, one step down from a full scholarship. By then he had stopped molesting her and she returned to reading books like *Lolita* and *Naked Lunch*.

And when Esther went abroad to study she put him out of her mind. At least, so she thought.

He came back with a coaster and water in a frosted square glass. Many things about his appearance had changed since she last saw him. His head was now bald and his gait was fluid to the point of being almost delicate. He had on loose fitting cream linen pants and a floppy white shirt, which appeared to be sizes too large by intention. His salt-and-pepper beard was well-manicured. When he handed over the water, she couldn't help but notice how neat and clean his nails were.

"Do you know how old I was?"

"Thirteen."

"And you were thirty-five."

"Thirty-three." He pause. "I wouldn't have touched you if…"

"If what?"

He leaned forward to cup his drink in his large hands. He held it for a while as if it were some kind of talisman.

"If… If I knew… Look, it's not like I was the first one. You told me about that other boy."

"I made that up. But even if there was another boy. So what? That still didn't give you the right."

He retreated to the sliding doors that looked out onto the beach. With a gentle tug, he slid them open. Balmy air slipped in. His shirt billowed. She felt the hair on her arm respond to the chill.

He turned. "If I knew…"

"Stop saying that!"

"It has bothered me, too."

"Bothered you? Is that what you think I am? Bothered?"

"I wouldn't have thought that until today." He picked up his drink again and stared into it. "Both you and Kevin have lived up to all my expectations. Look at Kevin. His achievement has been astounding. He's perhaps the only black Barbadian who owns a chain of hotels throughout the Caribbean. And you. I was so impressed when your mother told me that you had become a doctor. She was really very proud of you. But she couldn't understand why you never stayed with her when you came back to the island."

"I was haunted."

"By what?"

"Everything. Everything about that house. Everything about that village."

He eased into a plush chair near the door and crossed his legs. "Ashamed of where you came from?"

"Nothing that provocative. Ashamed of being me."

"Why?"

"Do you need to ask that?"

"You don't like your job?"

"It has it's rewards."

"Your mother said you were a surgeon."

"I spend my days remaking other people's bodies. Cutting away their ugliness. Helping them to redefine themselves. Like I said. It has its rewards. Some of the people who come to me are very beautiful. Yet they're not happy with the way they look. Sometimes I want to tell them to go look at themselves again. Some truly need my service and I'm glad to help them."

She paused. A question rushed to her mind. It jolted her. He saw the look in her eyes.

"What?"

She couldn't bring herself to ask the question. The answer now most certainly would be irrelevant. Or would it? She would want to think so, but distressingly, she wasn't sure.

She must've known then that she wasn't the most beautiful creature in the world. Her nose was probably too wide to have been considered *nice* by most Bajans. She was short, with thick, stubby legs. But she felt like the most beautiful creature in the world when he told her so. Esther wondered if that was why he picked her. To a man of his worldliness, it must've been obvious that she was self-conscious about her body. The way most 13-year-olds are. That was not the case anymore. After many years as a cosmetic surgeon she had come to realize that the only classic body is the one you own.

She has also learned that in the world of seduction, the laws of physical attraction are rooted in the distortion of reality. If only she knew that back then. In their world, his hunger for power got fuel from her pubescent need for validation.

And in this distorted reality she fell under his spell. There was his mastery with language; so seductive to her young, inquisitive mind. Add that to the sheer power of his physical presence, which seemed to will her to recklessness. He convinced her that anything was possible. Even becoming a doctor. But she must've known it was wrong even then for she remembered that many times after he'd used her body she would be unable to sleep at night.

"You manipulated me. You made me do things that to this day still haunts me. I didn't know what I was doing."

"That's nonsense."

"You took my innocence from me."

"That is so cliché." He unfolded his legs and then folded them again. Very slowly. It seemed to follow the speed of his thinking. He spoke in a quieter, more controlled voice. "In my view innocence is so overrated."

"Did someone do it to you?"

"What? Take my innocence?" He laughed.

"Those years were not meant for you. You took them. You stole them. And I can't figure out why. Why did you do it?"

"You could've stopped anytime you wanted to."

"You wouldn't let me go. I tried to get away. I was no match for your sweet talk."

"That's not how I remember it. You were very precocious sexually for a thirteen-year-old."

"Talk about cliché?" My God! You fed me books like *Tropic of Cancer*. Then you took advantage of my confusion."

"If I remember correctly, you'd already read *The Story of O*. Come on. Your brother told me you used to stay up late reading with your hands between your legs."

"My brother? My brother told you... You can't be serious." She paused, trying to control her anger. "How would Kevin know that?"

"Didn't you share a room at some point?"

He was right about her sharing a room with Kevin. It was during that yeasty period of her life when her body was changing rapidly and she spent a great deal of time confused and moody. Her mother was living in a world of memories and regret, unable to overcome her husband's death. Esther wrote a lot of lurid poetry in those days. She was a restless bird, eager, yet afraid of everything around her. Nothing was real to her. And yet, everything was so gravid with emotion.

After Esther's father died, her mother would never let Kevin out of her sight. He slept in her bed until he was almost nine. That's when he was displaced by a bandy-legged bartender her mother met at the hotel where she worked. Finally, a man to replace her husband. But that relationship soured and Kevin went back to sleeping in their mother's room.

Bishop got up wearily. "What is this all about?"

"It's about what you took from me."

"And you think I can give it back now?"

"I belong to a running group in Philadelphia. A group of women. One evening, one of the woman polled the rest of us about our first kiss. It was an innocent enough question. When did you have your first kiss? The kind of question women ask each other when they get to an age where regret can play tricks on memory. When they got to me I couldn't answer. What was I going to say? My tutor taught me how to kiss when I was thirteen. It wasn't a memory I wanted to share. I was ashamed. I knew they would laugh at me. That they would look at me with pity. Because the pain would've been on my face. I wished I could've shared that moment. I wished I had a moment to share. They were all happy and giggling. Except me. I couldn't share. I missed out."

"It's not how you felt then."

"How do you even know how I felt then or at any other time? You weren't interested in my feelings then. And it's clear you still aren't. Do you know what I've been through over the years? Three failed marriages. Two pregnancies that I couldn't go through with."

"You can't blame me for that. I'm not responsible for your bad choices. How the hell can you blame me for that. Look at where you are today. You think you would've done all this without the work I did with you?"

"So that's why you did it? You were exacting payment. Wasn't my mother enough?"

There was a long pause. The haughty glow was gone from his face. His eyes and lips stiffened, and the droop of flesh beneath his jaw grew.

She continued, "I found out just before I left the island. That she paid for our lessons with her body."

"Why don't you let sleeping dogs lie?"

"I tried that. It doesn't work. Not when the dog had infected you with fleas."

"I didn't make the arrangement. She did."

Esther threw the glass across the room. "You bastard!"

He tried to duck out of the way but it got him on his left shoulder then broke on the floor.

Meticulously, he picked up the pieces of shattered glass and then walked over to her with the same deliberateness. The biggest piece he held in one hand. She saw a red speck on his thumb. He'd cut himself.

Panic seized her when he got within reach. His eyes were steady and hard.

She tried not to show her fear. The determination to finish what she started fell on her hard. "Did she also arrange for you to abuse me?"

"You want to know why I did it? It's really quite simple. You were there. I could have you. I could have you and there would be no consequences. I can't say I'm sorry I did it now because at the time I did it with a clear mind. Without reservations."

"Aren't you sorry about what you did to me?"

"I'm sorry about hurting you. Is that what you wanted to hear?"

"You don't mean it. I wanted to come here and be able to forgive you. Because this anger I feel is a blight on my soul. I have to let it go. I thought that you could help me release it. But you can't. You can't. And that's sad. People say you're doing nice things. But you're not a nice man. You don't regret what you did to me. I hate you. I will always hate you. But at least now I know you deserve it. You don't think it was wrong. And you're not worthy of forgiveness."

She left fighting back tears. No closure to be had here. Why did she think it was possible? Life and its messiness. How can one endure them without sentimentality? She walked down to the end of the street before letting the tears come.

It took about fifteen minutes for her to regain her composure. And then she realized that she hadn't call Mort to pick her up. She reached for her cell phone. Lights from an approaching car momentarily blinded her. It drove by slowly. As it passed, she glanced inside the back of the taxi and her eyes made four with Kevin's.

i heard about her death from a friend of a friend. It had come up in passing, during a conversation we were having over pudding and souse at Culpeppers on Nostrand Avenue. This friend of a friend, who I'd met only days before, saw me sitting alone and offered her company. I accepted. We began to speak of this and that, of the old country, Barbados, when she casually asked if I knew this woman by name. Solace Mangrove.

"She's from the same village you come from," the woman said.

"Yes, I know her."

"Was she a friend of yours?"

"You could say that. Why?"

"She died."

The report of Solace's death set my heart fluttering. "Died?"

"It was in the Nation newspaper. Some man stoned her to

death. What kind of man would stone a woman to death?"

The shock must've been obvious on my face.

The woman reached over and touched my hand. "I'm sorry."

Quite apart from the horror of hearing about the death of someone you knew, someone who was still a young person, I realized that this news cleaved to my bosom in a way I could not fathom, and for the rest of the evening I was unable to think of anything else. I was perplexed as to why I felt such a sense of loss. Why did Solace's death devastate me so?

We grew up not more than three houses apart on a hill overlooking canefields and the sea. From our houses we could see the Atlantic Ocean and the fishing boats as they went out in the morning. And on that hill we played hopscotch, hide-and-seek, brown-girl-in-the-ring, hiddy-biddy and rounders together as children. I would like to say I knew her well. The truth was, I didn't. Her father had abandoned the family shortly after Solace was born forcing Solace's mom to seek greener pastures in London. Solace and two older sisters were left in the care of their grandmother. Many years later I found out that the man we thought was Solace's father wasn't really her father, and that was the reason he left. Solace's father had been a white English sailor her mother had met somewhere in the city.

I wanted to remember Solace as the beautiful girl of my youth. The lissome brown-skinned girl who set tongues wagging and eyes popping whenever she skipped through the village. The blithe spirit whose entrancing beauty overpowered any game we played. Especially brown-girl-in-the-ring.

There's a brown girl in the ring
Tra la la la la
There's a brown girl in the ring

Tra la la la la
There's brown girl in the ring
Tra la la la la
And she looks like a sugar and a plum plum
Girl show me your motion
Tra la la la la
Girl show me your motion
Tra la la la la
And she looks like a sugar and a plum plum

When we played brown-girl, everyone tried to make sure they got a turn in the ring before Solace. After Solace became the girl in the ring, the game would come to an end. For how could anyone match Solace's beauty?

I'd seen her several times while on vacation back on the island no more than three years ago and had been shocked by the deterioration of that beauty. Most of her teeth had fallen out, her face had shrunk, her eyes soulless. She was barely thirty years old.

When we were growing up Solace's long wavy hair and olive skin was the envy of all the girls in the village. Amidst the glory of bright sunshine and beaches cast in perfection, our tropical isle hung its shoulders under the heavy burden of a social pecking order left over from slavery.

White on top.
Light-brown down one rung.
Brown still further down.
Black on the ground.

The kind of envy this created in an island that was a crucible of poverty was long lasting, dividing and destroying families, setting villages at war with each other.

And so it was in Solace's family and in our village. As early as the age of twelve, she became an object of desire to many men. This did not go unnoticed by her older sisters and dark-skinned peers in the village who took delight in spreading whatever rumor about Solace they make up, no matter how petty.

The onset of puberty and the attention it drew to Solace from boys and men in the village alike, brought a halt to our child-hood play. Her precocious physical development was now the talk of the village and it was clear that her body had outgrown our youthful games, as her grandmother tried to keep the jewel of Solace's virginity beyond the grasp of ordinary men.

However, this did not stop me from dreaming about her. This did not keep me from strolling by her house in the evening hoping to get a glimpse of her sitting in the window, since she was no longer allowed to play with us. She became a fixture in my adolescent fantasies, and any sighting of Solace, whether on the school bus, or walking along the street was enough to keep me up exploring in my mind the wonderful possibilities of being her boyfriend.

At fifteen she got pregnant and dropped out of school. It was downhill for Solace from there.

The identity of the child's father shocked every one in the village. The man was a known thief and liar. He was often unemployed, drank a lot, gambled away what little money he made when he worked and was violent. In his youth he lived in our village, moving away to live in the city after a short stint in a reform school for boys. The whole village wanted to know how he managed to scale her grandmother's walls to enter Solace's pearly gates.

Many years later, Solace confided to me that the seduction began and ended with his mouth.

"He had these bountiful thick lips. They looked so soft.

Like purple clouds. And when he talked to me I always felt like he should be kissing me instead of talking."

"Were you in love with him?" I asked.

"No, I don't think so. Nor he with me."

"You just liked his lips?" I asked.

"Yes, and he was different. Not like most men. He didn't seem to be caught up in the way I looked. And that was the challenge. I wanted to make him want me like everybody else."

After she got pregnant her family practically disowned her. They built her a little shack on property they owned and left her to attend to her own affairs. They were a proud bunch, the Mangroves, and like the rest of the village had expected her to be a jewel, a prize worthy of a white man, or some wealthy foreigner. Certainly beyond the reach of anybody in our village. Maybe they warned Solace that some challenges are not worth pursuing and she ignored them. Either way, with a child at sixteen, she was now tarnished in their eyes.

Unemployed and undereducated in a county where men often preyed on young soft-minded girls, Solace was easy pickings, as she sought to keep her child clothed and fed. Appealing to her family was little use. Many days her child ate only stolen fruit.

A series of low-paying jobs did nothing to improve her situation. In fact, they only made life worse. Wherever she worked, there was always some supervisor or manager, who, looking to claim her as a prize, framed his demand by insinuating that keeping her job depended on her compliance with his sexual needs. Desperate to keep food on the table and a roof over her head, Solace gave into many such advances. The beauty that many thought would've been her ticket to an easy life had become a curse.

I graduated high school and began enjoying life as an adult, staying out late to revel in the spoils of my first job. One night, coming home from the movies, I saw Solace on the bus. By this time her reputation had been ripped to shreds by the dogs of gossip and scattered about the dirt roads of our village. She had started to drink and had had another child. Words like *whore* and *slut* were the stones of verbal abuse she dodged daily as she tried to scrape enough to feed her children.

She got off the crowded bus ahead of me and was already ten yards down the road by the time I made it off. The rhythmic *plap-slap* of her slippers echoed in the night. Hung low above us was a rich black sky empty of light except for a few distant stars spread out like lost sheep.

"Hey, Yellow-girl," I called out.

Yellow-girl was her nickname. Shoulders hunched, head down, she quickened her pace.

I'd had a few beers with some friends after the movie and was feeling quirky. I ran up next to her and fell into stride, shoulder to shoulder.

She turned to look at me briefly, but said nothing. Her white shirt was pink-streaked, the result, I assumed, of a liquid spill. The pink blotches and lines looked like the work of a tie-dye artist. Solace was breathing heavy, her chest heaving and convulsing rapidly.

"Are you okay, Solace?"

She nodded without looking at me.

"Where you coming from?" I asked.

Instead of answering she began to walk even faster, her slippers slapping angrily against the road as if tapping out a Morse code of resistance against my inquisitiveness.

Realizing she wasn't interested in talking, I hung back, gradually letting her move ahead. When I'd copped enough space to lick my wounds I began to whistle my favorite tune: *Papa Was a Rolling Stone.*

Then Solace stopped up ahead. I didn't even realize it until I caught up. With my pride almost safely tucked back into my pants, I was prepared to walk by as if she was an empty shirt blowing in the night breeze. She reached out and touched my bare arm.

Her palm was wet, her touch electric. The shock made me tremble. Before I could speak she smiled. Her face was pinched; her lips shivered. Heavy lids hid her eyes.

"You gotta go home right now?" Her voice broke at the word *home* and she started to cry.

"What's the matter?" Here was my chance to ingratiate myself

"Nothing. I just don't feel like being by myself."

"You want me to come home with you?"

"Please." Her eyes opened wide. I could feel her fingers digging into my skin.

"You sure you okay?"

"I just don't feel like being alone tonight."

her house was dark and smelled of ripe paw-paw. She lit a lamp in one room, which seemed to serve as kitchen, living room and dining room. The other room facing a field of canes was the bedroom. The windows were closed and the humidity prickled my skin.

I was surprised to see the children asleep in the bedroom. The older one, a boy, slept on the floor; the girl, was asleep on the bed.

"You leave them here by themselves," I whispered.

"Stephen is very good with Mavis. He look after her good. He's a little man you see him there."

"He's about four now, right?"

"Four and a half."

"And her?" I pointed at the baby in the bed. "I remember when she was born. She's two."

She looked at me with a half smile of surprise. And then she laughed in a carefree way, as if we'd just discovered some new secret together.

"What you wanna do?" My voice trembled. I was still dazed by the quickness of this conquest. I'd dreamed of this moment for so long.

"I don't know. Just lie down. I'm tired."

"Just lie down?" I was caught unawares and my disappointment tumbled out.

"What do you want to do?"

"Well, I just don't wanna lie down, yuh know. We could do something."

"Like what?" What you wanna do?"

Yuh know, I thought. Well... I thought. I don't know. I don't just want to lie down."

"You want to foop me?"

I was startled by her bluntness. "I ain't saying that's what I want. I mean... it ain't all I want. But, if you want."

"We could do that if that's what you want."

The note of resignation in her voice troubled me, though not enough to keep me from kissing her. Her lips were stiff. Not at all what I expected. I had to force my tongue past her clenched teeth. My hand dropped to her skirt and found its way underneath, wandering up her leg into the meat of her hot thighs and beyond the boundary of her panties. Her pubic hair was thick and sweaty. She stood rigid, like someone being robbed. I was lost in the fantasy and took little note of her lack of interest. When I tried to push a finger inside her she recoiled with a low squeal, her face scrawled with lines of fear.

"I can't," she cried.

"Please!"

"I'm sorry. I can't."

"You don't know how many nights I dreamed about you," I pleaded.

"It too sore."

"What you mean it too sore?"

She pulled away. "You don't know what too sore mean?"

She left me there and went into the bedroom. I watched as she made space on the floor next to the little boy, then gently lifted the sleeping girl from the bed and placed her softly on the bedding.

She took off her skirt, leaving her blouse on. I stood staring at her thick calves and then at a dark blotch on her leg, feeling uneasy, not sure whether to leave or invite myself into the bedroom.

Wearily she eased herself onto the bed, curling into a ball like a cat.

A knot grew in my belly. I wasn't sure if it was anger at the way she walked away, or from the quiet understanding that Solace was in pain and I was pitifully unprepared to help.

"Come and lie down with me," she said.

I stood there as if my feet were nailed to the scabrous floor. There was a pale glow seeping through a crack above the window behind me.

"What's the matter?" she said.

"It's too hot," I said.

"Take off your clothes."

Not knowing what else to do, I obeyed. First my pants, then my shirt. Keeping my briefs on, I tiptoed across the floor, every creak of the floorboard echoing the pangs of regret I was feeling.

She slid over and waited for me to settle down next to her. The bed was worn, lumpy in spots and smelled of mildew and urine. With her back to me, she fitted her broad hips into the curve of my loins. Her skin was remarkably cool.

"Thanks," she said.

I remained silent, breathing the shallow breath of a man recognizing a mistake, but unable to change course.

"I'm sorry I can't let you foop me," she whispered. "It en that I don't want you to. I like you. Always did. You was always nice to me."

"So why you so sore down there?"

It en important. You wouldn't understand." She paused. "You vex?"

"No, I en vex. It en like you promise me nutten."

"You's such a nice boy."

"So what happen that it so sore?"

"I was by my boyfriend. I wanted to come home to my kids. He wanted me to stay. I say no. When I try to leave he hold me down and foop me real rough. I was bleeding."

"You mean he rape you?"

"He's my boyfriend."

"Why you stay with somebody like that?"

I sat up to look at her. She turned to face me, her eyes red and tired.

"You deserve a good man," I said.

She laughed. "A good man? Where would I find a good man? You?"

"If you was my woman. . ."

"Yes. If I was your woman. . .What would you do?"

"You too good for a man like that," I said.

"You wouldn't know what to do with a woman like me," she said.

"I wouldn't rape you. I wouldn't foop you so rough."

"What you know 'bout women? Maybe I like getting foop rough. You's a boy. You en know nutten 'bout women. I bet you's still a virgin."

"And you's a slut."

The thought flew from my mouth before I could eat it. Certainly wasn't what I'd meant to say. But her admonishment had stung. I was nineteen years. We were the same age. How could she call me a boy? And how did she know I'd never been with a woman?

"You think I's a slut?" Her face was calm and composed.

"No, I don't think that. I didn't mean it that way."

"Yes, you did. Everybody does." She turned away. "You know what though. I don't care."

She turned to look at me again, but only for a second. There was a hint of sadness at the edge of her eyes then it was gone. She curled up again into a ball and fifteen minutes later she was asleep.

The incipient anger at not getting the chance to fulfill my fantasy subsided, undermined by pity. And then I decided that I must be in love with her because I wanted her to wake up so I could beg her forgiveness. Through the night I stayed awake, not sure what to do. I couldn't sleep. Filled with shame, I crept out of the house just before dawn. She was right. I was still just a boy because a man would've confessed his love given that chance.

We did not speak of the incident after that. Indeed we hardly spoke before I left the island some four years later. It was not that we avoided each other, but when we happened to see one another, however infrequently it occurred, we simply smiled, said hello and went our way. Whenever it seemed that something else approximating a real conversation might develop one of us would cast a sheepish look downward, eating up the ground with our eyes, unable to make the opportunity last.

By the time I left the island Solace had had two more children and her teeth had begun to fall out. She was no longer what you would call pretty and spent most of her time drinking in a run-down shack called the Palace.

For some reason, I felt compelled to attend her funeral. As I packed my suitcase, I thought about that night I almost slept with Solace. It wasn't the first time I thought about that night. Many times over the years I've pondered her question: *What would you do if I was your woman?*

Could I have saved her? I guess I'll never know.

LICKS LIKE PEAS

it did just after she seventeenth birthday that Sonia meet
Adolphus Carter, or Pigeon, as most people does call he, a
tall, broad-back man who did 'bout ten years older than she.
Pigeon did just move to Pilgrim Road to live in a house he
uncle did gone to the States and leave him.

If you know Pilgrim Road, this uncle used to live right
below the mini-mart, which was right across the street from
the bus stop. The very same bus stop, if you remember, where
Arelene Pounder strip off all of Diane Payne's clothes after
some malicious body tell Arlene that Diane was pregnant fuh
Arlene boyfriend. Make poor Diane run home naked. And
the hurtful thing is yuh coulda see that Diane was showing
already. Ah mean, suppose she did make that girl fall down

and lose she baby! That is why when Arlene get in that accident in the mini-bus and lose all she front teeth nobody din
feel sorry fuh she at all.

Anyhow, Sonia get off the bus at that said bus stop one
evening as Pigeon was washing he brand new Corolla by the
side of the road. Now Pigeon is one a them bodybuilder
fellas and he love showing off, so he out there bareback in
shorts. And he dark, dark. So, the muscles glistening in the
sun. He stop Sonia with a broad smile on he smooth face,
with teeth shining like rainwater on a crapaud back.

"Girl, I got something to tell you," he saying.

She pretending not to notice how he looking at she
woman-size legs in the uniform that she grandmother always
telling her she was too short for school.

"But this is how all my friends does dress," Sonia would
counter.

"So if all you friends jump in a well, you would jump in it
behind them?" the grandmother reply.

"You don't know nutten, Ma."

And with that, her grandmother would mime zipping her
own mouth shut and the conversation would end.

"You en got nutten to tell me that I waan hear," Sonia
saying to Pigeon. But she still slowing down just in case he
decide to follow she.

"I going to make you my wife, yuh know." he saying.

She start to laugh and didn't even bother to turn back to
look at him.

That night she looking out she window at the far away
stars thinking 'bout how she going soon leave the island to
live wid she mother in Florida. She eager to get back to the
States where she was born. When she was seven, her Bajan

mother send she to Barbados to live with her grandmother. Partly because she was working two jobs and finding somebody to care for Sonia was a big headache, but also because she believe Sonia would get a better primary and secondary education in Barbados.

Every summer Sonia would head north to be with she Mom who recently relocated from the Bronx to Orlando. And now that she about to finish high school she would be going back to America for good. Sonia had never been to Disneyworld. She was looking forward to that. And going to the zoo. She loved the zoo. One of the high points of spending summers in New York was going to the Bronx zoo. Her mother said the zoo in Orlando was even better than the one in New York.

She was anxious for some excitement right now, though. Life in Barbados was boring as shite; with the tight leash her grandmother keeping her on, the only excitement she getting is the late night thrill of reading the lastest book by Zane which she'd been milking for a month now. Her mother was far more liberal. In Orlando, Sonia knew she'd be allowed to go on dates, something her grandmother believes only grow on trees.

But in the background, Pigeon words buzzing sweet in she ear.

I going to make you my wife, yuh know.

The man crazy, though. He didn't even know nutten 'bout she. Still the words got she smiling. Maybe it was because he sounded so sure 'bout heself. Not like the little pissy boys who always pulling at she in the school bus, or the unemployed limers down by the mini-mart who always *sissing* at she like they calling puppies.

It en even that she was taking wuh he say seriously. She was smarter than that. He was a man after all.

Sonia figured she'd already learnt everything she needed to know about men from her aunt, Maxine, a self-professed man-expert. According to Maxine, men will lie and sweet-talk a woman just for a taste what Maxine called 'the sauce.' Once they get a taste, even before they swallow good, they off looking for another pot to lick.

Growing up in a house with Maxine, she watched how her aunt exploited men's addiction to the sauce. Though Maxine wasn't what Bajans would call pretty, she always had men knocking down she door. Maxine was a downright tease. She promised and promised but the men never seemed to get tired of begging. Bajan men persistent, yuh hear!

Men are easily manipulated, Maxine would say. Tease them and they will be your slaves. Don't ever give in. Keep promising until you get what you want and then go your merry way.

Sonia suspected Maxine was that way because she grow up hearing people making nuff, nuff joke 'bout she big lips and she boar-cat eyes. Yuh know how Bajans could be. She was so desperate fuh somebody to nice she that when the butcher from next door went from playing wid she braids and patting she backside to putting he hand under she skirt she en do nutten to stop him, though her twelve-year-old sense tell she it was wrong.

When she mother found out she cornroast Maxine backside wid a tamarind rod, and call her stupid. From then Maxine decide no man would ever get to take advantage of her again.

So it en like Sonia believe Pigeon. Even so, what he say still make she feel good. Maxine was always telling she to watch out for sweet-talking men, but she din explain that there's men that talk sweet, and then there's men that does drop syrup from their mouth. That it en what a man say but how he say it. If he saying things just because he got a mout or if he saying it like he could make it happen.

She reasoned, though, it would be better to ignore Pigeon and he sweet-talk. Still what harm could there be in walking down by the mini-mart just about the time she know he liked to wash his car?

Which is exactly what she did two days later. He stop to watch she walk by but didn't say nutten. She walk past a few yards and stop.

"You en going to speak to me?" she said, turning around.

"Evenin."

"Evenin? That is all you got to say to me?"

She started to walk away.

"Listen," he saying. "I could pass by Queens College on my way to work, yuh know. If you want a lift to school tomorrow just come down the gap before eight."

"Where you does work?"

"I's guard the prisoners at Glendairy. And one day I gine guard you love with my life."

later that night she trying to read Love's Labor's Lost for school. But she can't concentrate. She reading Shakespeare's pentameter and hearing Pigeon's cooing. And for some strange reason she studying his offer seriously. The bus does always be crowded in the morning. And hot. And smelly. It would be nice to get to school without somebody crushing her neatly pressed skirt, or somebody stepping on her brightly polished shoes. It would be nice to get to school on time, looking fresh as a morning glory. She wondering wuh Maxine would do. She even thinking 'bout picking up the phone and calling Maxine in St. Lucia.

Next morning she walk down the gap and stand up next to the car waiting fuh Adolphus to come out. When he come out she open the passenger door and get in without even saying nutten. Not one word. No reason to give him any ideas.

As they driving down the road she wondering why he en trying to talk to she, throwing she some sweet-talk she way. But Pigeon mouth zip. Not a word. By the time they reach in front the school she so vex she get out and slam the door as hard as she could.

That evening she en see him washing the car. But later, about eight o'clock on her way back from the mini-mart where she went to get bread to make lunch, she see him standing on his front step.

"Evenin," he say, stepping down into the street.

"I en talking to you," she bark.

"Wuh I do?"

"You know good and well wuh you do."

"You mean this mornin?" He smile and his eyes open wide. "Girl to tell the truth I did frighten to open me mouth. I din know what to say. I was so overwhelmed sitting that close to you. You so beautiful I feel like I did sitting next to an African queen. You had me head kurfuffle then. I just wanted to enjoy the feeling of being that close to you."

She smiled. Boy he could talk sweet though.

"You got a minute?" he say. "I got something inside to show you."

"What?"

"It en gine take long."

She look up the street to make sure she granny wasn't coming down and then she follow Pigeon inside his house. The place did furnish off nice. He pick up a silk blouse from a chair.

"My sister in New York send me some things to sell, but I take one look at this and I say this make fuh you."

She run she hand over the blouse. "It beautiful. How much it cost?"

"Fuh you? Nothing. A gift."

She didn't know what to say. Other than her parents nobody never give she nutten so beautiful before. She stand up like she rooted to the floor, staring at Pigeon almond-shape eyes. And the way he smiling starting to do something to she, like it starting to hypnotize she. He en too bad looking though, she thinking. And he got nice eyes too. And he so big and strong. Like he could hold up a house pon he shoulders.

She en even realize that he now holding she face in he hand. She start thinking she should leave when he lean down and kiss she so long she nearly stop breathing.

It feel like somebody light a match under she skirt. She knees start to buckle, and if he din hold she up, she woulda collapse to the floor.

As she lay in she bed later than night, she still feeling exhilarated and strangely ashamed at the things she let Pigeon do to she. Ashamed that she enjoy them so much. She beginning to wonder if all the things Maxine tell she 'bout men was really true. How come Maxine never tell she that a man could touch yuh body and make yuh feel so sweet yuh won't care if the world end right then. Pigeon seemed to know exactly what would drive she crazy. Where to put he mouth. Where to lick. Like if he had control of her mind.

She couldn't keep away after that. Yuh shoulda hear some the excuses she coming up to sneak off to Pigeon's house.

Hear she.

"Ma, all the ice-cream gone. I hot. I want something to cool me off. I going up by the mini-mart and get some icecream."

"But I just buy icecream yesterday," The grandmother saying.

"I en like that kind. That kind too soft."

Or this one.

"Ma, how come you only buy the short hotdogs? You know I like the long ones, too. I gine up by the mini-mart and get some."

"But since when is long hotdogs you like?"

"Since I get some at school the other day. Them does keep you full longer than the short ones."

Or this classic.

"Ma, where the milk? You know I like to drink milk at night. It does help me sleep. I gine by the mini-mart and get milk."

"But, girl, you en see milk in the fridge? her granny start protesting. "You must be blind."

Wuh yuh think she say?

"I en like that kind now. That is low-fat milk. I prefer whole milk"

Every time she granny back turn Sonia tek off fuh Pigeon house. After graduation Sonia gave up all pretence and despite her grandmother's objection that it was scandalous for a girl so young to be sleeping with a hardback man, she became a fixture in Pigeon's house. Day and night.

The grandmother was the happiest woman in Pilgrim Road when Sonia's plane ticket come. She pack Sonia off to Florida faster than you could say Tom Pigeon.

but even in Florida Sonia can't get Pigeon off she mind. She feeling out of place in at Disneyworld. She no longer liked the zoo. It was a place for children. She was a woman now. The zoo was crowded and noisy, and not as much fun as she remembered. Maybe the animals in Florida din like to be stared at. They looked tired and bored.

Every chance she get she calling Barbados. And is bare sweet-talk she getting from Pigeon who reading love poems he find in a book to she over the phone, and telling she that if she don't come back he might just walk in the sea and don't look back.

"Girl, as soon as you come back we gine get married at Sandy Lane."

And she believe he too.

So when she mother notice the low grades she getting in the college where she was studying accounting, she sit Sonia down and give she a long speech.

"You just turn eighteen. You too young to be pining behind a man. You need to focus on yuh future. Yuh in America now. What ever you want to do in life yuh can do it here. And I will do whatever I can do to help you. But yuh need to fuhget 'bout this man in Barbados. En nothing he can do for you. Barbados can't give you the opportunities you can get here. If you can't fuhget 'bout this man then you may is well go long back, cause I tired paying three and four hundred dollars every month in phone bills."

That was all Sonia needed to hear. A month later, she was back in Barbados cock up like a queen in Adolphus house.

as far as Sonia concern, her mother couldn'ta been more wrong. Barbados had everything she wanted because all she wanted was to hear Pigeon cooing in she ear at night. She was in love and it was the sweetest thing she ever tasted. Life was almost perfect. Pigeon giving she everything she ask for and more. And even though she wanted to work he telling she that he making good money in the prisons and that all she had to do was stay sweet for him.

For a while that was fine. But it only take she six months to get bored with doing nothing. All she doing is putting on weight. And she can't get Adolphus to set a date for the wedding. He giving she all kinda excuse. He looking to buy a house first. How it go look fuh them to get married and still living in he uncle house? He want to pay off the car note first. How it going look if he having big wedding and still owing the bank for a car?

A year pass and still no date fuh the wedding. Eighteen months. All this easy living got she getting too plump fuh she liking. Clothes can't fit. The more weight she put on, the bigger the smile on Pigeon face. Every day he telling she how good she looking.

"Girl, you look like a ripe breadfruit!"

But she don't like the way everything on she body bouncing like she in a minibus on a rough road. And she hating all the unwanted attention from men who watching she like a mongoose does watch chicken. Like she is tonight's dinner. All she want is for Adolphus to keep the promises that get she to leave Florida.

He en know how many people telling she that she shtupid fuh leaving America to come back and live wid a prison guard? Her friend Sherma get on bad when she hear that Sonia was back in Barbados.

"Girl, I have five minds not to speak to you ever again. Wuh you must be born on the thirtieth of February. Nuhbody can't be that shtupid. Dah tommie he got must be got gold pon um, cause that's the only way I woulda make a decision like that. And it would got to be gold that I could scrape off an' sell whenever I want."

Perhaps she was a shameless romantic. Was there something wrong wid wanting to spend yuh life wid the man who take your virginity? Was there something wrong wid wanting to love one man forever?

But she beginning to realize that Pigeon sweet talk is like soap bubbles. Soon as it hit the air, it disappear. He en really eager to relinquish his bachelorhood. Live-wid wasn't her idea of marriage. She didn't care that it was an accepted Bajan way of setting up house.

fed up with the drudgery of cooking and cleaning she get a job as a receptionist at Casuarina hotel. She was very excited about working. Finally, something to keep she mind occupied. Talk about a perfect fit. She take to the job like a crab to a swamp. Two-Two's so, she had a promotion to the accounts department.

She loving that the job was near the beach, too. At least an hour every day, she would spend outside enjoying the beauty of the area, which went far beyond the acrylic blue sea. The hotel had lush vegetation all around. Every day she would just marvel at the way the green plants shimmer in the cool breezes blowing off the sea. It was the time of year for sea-grape trees and the trees did full of fruit. She get one of the young boys who used to hang 'bout the hotel to pick some of the tart-sweet fruit fuh she to eat on the way home.

This one afternoon, she did standing on the edge of the beach just watching the waves lollygag up to the sand. Egrets gliding cross the sky like the red-hot sun got them dazed. Such a soothing sight. She din want to leave, but it was time for she to go back to work. She turn round and almost bump into him standing with another man.

"Hi," he said.

"Oh, sorry. Din even see nobody standing behind me."

"Actually we been here for a while." He smiled. His teeth were slightly crooked, but his eyes bright and friendly. "What's your name?"

She thinking 'bout not responding directly, of playing the little cat and mouse game she love to play. But, then she see a kinda earnestness in he face that squashed the thought.

"Sonia."

He stretch out he right hand. "I'm Sylvan. This is my friend Tallabo."

Tallabo she accustom seeing 'round the hotel with different white women. He was hard to miss. Big as a mahogany tree and a man of few words. Rumor had it that Tallabo had spent some time in prison in the States for stabbing a man over a woman. Sylvan, she'd never seen before. She put she hand in he own, and she liked the way it swallowed hers up. But he din try to overwhelm she with his strength. She hated showoffs who grip yuh hand like they want to break it off. His hands were strong though, she could tell.

And then for some reason she eyes drifting to he lips and she find sheself thinking about what kind of kisser he would be. Embarrassed by the thought she quickly pull away and walk off without another word.

Two weeks pass before she see him again. The same place at around the same time. He had on shorts, floppy T-shirt, slip-on sandals and very dark glasses. When he smile his expanding lips reflecting in the mirror of his glasses. She couldn't stop looking at his lips.

"Is there something wrong?" he said.

"No, I was just. . . admiring your glasses."

"Rayban. The best."

"They must be very warm."

"Warm?"

"I mean, they must be keep your face hot. They are so dark and thick."

"Thick?"

"They look thick. . ."

"How can you tell that?"

She smiled. Keep him guessing. They talked for about ten minutes about this and that. Where he live. Where she live. What kind of things they each liked to do. He liked to scuba dive and promised to take her one day. And so on and so forth. The usual preamble before the questions that induce heavy breathing.

"You wanna have dinner some time?" he asked.

"Dinner?"

Pigeon had never taken her out to dinner. Perhaps he talking 'bout Kentucky Fried Chicken or Cheffette.

"Dinner where?"

"At a restaurant," he replied softly.

"You mean like Kentucky?"

"No, I mean like Bajan Sugar."

"What it is you does do again?"

"I'm an entrepreneur?"

"Doing what?"

"Sales of arts and crafts. I have a gallery. I buy and sell local arts and craft."

"To who?"

"Mostly tourists."

"Buy low sell high?"

He laughed. "Where did you hear that expression."

"In America."

"Oh, you've traveled."

"Only to the States. You?"

"I've been all over. Seen all kinds of things. But I have to say never seen anything as beautiful as you."

Oh my goodness! Another sweet-talker.

They had dinner the next night at Bajan Sugar in St. Lawrence Gap. As she expected, Pigeon did breathing fire when she get home. But what surprise she was her indifference to it all. It didn't take much to shut him up. Telling him that she spent the evening walking along the beach thinking about whether or not she should stay with him since he didn't seem willing to marry her did the trick. He shut up one time so. Bram!

She was actually surprised that it work so well. Just like that, she now had the upper hand. She now had this power over Pigeon. He was afraid of her leaving, yet he would not marry her as promised. What kind of man would do that? It was this question she and her girlfriend Sherma trying to answer a few days later while waiting for the bus.

"Girl, I think it's an affliction bajan men get from breast-feeding too long," Sherma said

"You really think so." Sonia couldn't always tell when Sherma was being serious.

"Well, can you come up with a better explanation why bajan men so frighten fuh marriage?"

"To tell the truth I can't."

"Well, then. Breast-feeding too long is as good as any explanation. Dem spoiled. Sometimes yuh does have to put a horn or two in their tail to shake them up."

"You think so?"

"How yuh tink I get that man I had to put a ring on me finger?"

"You horn he?"

"Ring two good horns in he backside. Had he scotching. One wid a old boyfriend who knew his way around the yard. Just to make sure it wasn't going to be a waste of time. And then one wid a foreigner fella to make sure he didn't come back to cause nuh trouble later on down the road."

"And how you ex-husband react when he find out?"

"He get on like somebody cut out he heart." Sherma laughed like she was remembering. "He cry like a baby. Lord, ah did feel fuh he though. Ah din know it was gine brek he up so. He had to stay home from work for a week 'cause he did shakin suhmuch he did frighten he woulda cut off he own hand working on them machines."

"And you din frighten he do something shtupid like beat you or kill you. Yuh know these men 'bout here like to grab up cutlass like them think it is a kung fu movie them starring in."

"He know if he touch one hair on my head my brothers woulda un-make he rass."

"Hornin the man seem like a pretty drastic thing to do."

"Drastic? Don't mek me laugh. If you boss see you sleepin on the job, he en gine fire you?"

"I suppose."

"Would you call that drastic? When yuh mention marriage to a Bajan man he does get on like you threatening to cut out he stones."

Sonia laughed. "The thing is, Pigeon is the body bring the marriage talk to me first."

"But yuh know, is we fault. We give them that kinda power by gettin on like if we en get married we life en complete."

"Yuh got a point there. We should just live and enjoy we life. Man or no man. Marriage or no marriage. It ent every woman that got a man."

"Or want a man. I got a aunt in New York who is fifty-six and never had a man. Say she taking she virginity to Heaven. And she's the happiest person I know."

"I think I movin out," Sonia say. "I meet somebody that real nice. I want to try he out but I en want to horn Pigeon. Maybe you right. Maybe if Pigeon see me with somebody else he would realize I serious."

"If you goin move out why yuh don't take yuh tail back to the States?"

the next week she moved into her grandmother's house, which had been empty for about a year. When Sonia went back to the States her granny decide she din care to live alone and went to live in St. Lucia with Maxine.

Pigeon en put up no resistance because she suspect that he think she did bluffing. But when he come home that Friday night and find all she belongings gone, he got drunk and piss-parade out the front road. Talking 'bout how he glad she leave, and how he going have a different woman every night in the house, and how she would never get another man to treat she as nice as he.

The next morning you shoulda see he on he knees begging she to come back. She tell him she won't be coming back unless he show she a ring. He left she 'lone after that.

She meet Sylvan again for dinner two weeks later at the same restaurant. The man had so many interesting stories to tell. From his days traveling and performing limbo dance on a cruise ship to time spent in St. Thomas diving for sunken treasure, to managing a hotel in the forests of Suriname.

They talk until the place was ready to close. Then they move to a bar next door where she had one Margarita too many. By midnight, when them did ready to leave she had decided the night would be a complete disaster if she didn't make love to him. And she surprise sheself by revealing this to him.

Boy was she drunk!

He smile and shake he head. He like her a lot, he say. But, getting involved with her romantically would cause too much confusion.

Why? She want to know.

He was not the marrying type, he say, and he could tell that she was the kind of woman who looked for marriage.

This thing unsettled her for weeks. But hey, she never had no discussion 'bout marriage with the man. Why he would be saying that to she? Did she have the letter M stamp pon her forehead?

But his refusal to make love to her only stoking her competitive fire, not to mention her desire. They going dancing. Walking on the beach. They even kissing. But he would never accept any of her invitations inside the house when he drop her off afterward. Every night, after one of their dates, she going in she bed moister than a bajan black cake. And she having to get creative to relieve all this pressure.

After two months, she decide she couldn't take it anymore. That one way or another she going make it happen, even if she got to seduce him. She consulted Sherma about what kind of ruse she could use to get him inside the house. Once inside, the dog dead as the saying goes.

"First off," Sherma said, adjusting sheself on the narrow bench under the gooseberry tree below the bungalow that her husband built before Sherma kicked him out. "First, off, you sure this man is Bajan?"

"Yes. He born here. He does talk like a Bajan."

"Then he does play on the other side."

"You think so?"

"No Bajan man worth a bowl of coo-coo would turn down a woman that look as good as you. Girl, I's a woman and I would take a piece."

Sonia laugh out loud. "Sherma, girl stop making joke."

Sherma face serious. "Wuh make you think I joking?"

Sonia still laughing. "I en paying you nuh mind."

"Well, say that, but don't think I joking. I would put some good licks in you, girl."

Sonia look at Sherma to see if she could detect any clue that her friend was teasing. She couldn't, but decided she din want to continue that line of talk. "Fuh real, though. Tell me what I should do."

"You sure he en playing on the other side?"

"I don't think so, you know."

"He ever kiss you yet?"

"Yes. Plenty times."

"Wuh kinda kiss?"

"Wuh you mean?"

"A peck, like this?" Sherma puckered her lips. "Or a wet one."

Sonia closed her eyes, remembering the last time he kissed her. "Oh, wet. Very wet."

"Here's what you do the next time he bring you home. Tell him you hear there got a rapist loose in the village and you want him to come in the house with you to make sure there en nuhbody hiding inside."

"Yuh think he would fall fuh that?"

"I know Bajan men en got nuh reputation for bravery, but the only way he would refuse is if he know that somebody was actually in the house."

"Awright. I gine see if that work."

And work it did. Like a charm. He follow she inside like an obedient puppy and waited til she done turning on the light inside the house.

She take off all she clothes and call he inside the bedroom. That's all it take. Simple so. One look at she naked body and he fall down pon he knees like he praying. For the next hour he worship she with such hot kisses that she body was tingling from the heat it send surfing up through she belly like the first time she drink white rum. They made love til around 2 in the morning. Before the first cock crow he wake she up with light tongue-strokes on her inner thighs. She spread she legs open wide. Oh, what bliss! The people down in Durants musta hear she scream when he hit the magic spot. He kiss she one last time before leaving around 5:30.

She did just turn way from the door, latching it behind her new lover. A few steps back to the bedroom where she could lay down cross the bed again to daydream 'bout how he make love to she in a way that cause she voice to stop in the back of she throat.

She hear *Plax!*

Wuh dah could be?

Sonia sit up in the bed.

Plax! Plax!

Then she hear a scream that come through the house like hurricane wind. To this day she skin does still walk when she think 'bout that scream.

She run to the door and quick so unlatch it to peep outside. Wuh she see nearly give she heart attack.

Plax!

She got to the door just in time to see the fourth lash Pigeon throw at Sylvan. The thick clammy-cherry tree limb in Pigeon hand connected to Sylvan's shoulder. How Sylvan got off the ground before Pigeon could hit he again was a marvel. And the way he take off through the bush, not even Obadele coulda catch him.

Pigeon swing one more time and miss. The stick connect with the paling. *Brackalang!* The noise echoing like an explosion in the early morning. He take off after Sylvan but she know there wasn't much chance of him catching up with the younger man.

She scramble back to the bedroom, throw on a dress and jumped though the window just as Pigeon rush back into the house. You shoulda see she scampering through the backyard. Running through the tall grass to get to Sherma's house.

it was the talk of the village for weeks. How Pigeon catch she in bed with a man and share licks like peas. To she and the man. Nobody en mention how Pigeon turn up at Sherma house begging Sonia to come out to talk to he. Promising that if she come back he would marry she on the spot. She refuse to come out and Sherma threaten to call the police if he didn't leave.

Three days later she fled the island, boarding American Airlines for the land of her birth.

Sherma called Sonia in Orlando the next day. Pigeon show up that morning with a diamond ring and a reverend.

A week later Sherma call again.

"Girl, you en know Pigeon get stab up by a prisoner."

Sonia paused. "He dead?"

"Dead wuh? Scallywags like them so does dead? But guess where he get cut?"

"Where?"

Sherma laughed. "He going need a tube to pee. That is what I hear somebody at the bus stop saying."

TALL LIKE YOU

he had come up from one of those islands in the
Caribbean; Barbados it was, leaving behind a mother, three
sisters and cracked airless land. He came brimming with
confidence, with expectations heaped on him by family and
friends. By people who didn't even know him. That didn't
matter because he was going North. To the big city. Countless
others had made promises to come back rich. To send money.
Countless others had forgotten their promises. Became crim-
inals, strung out on drugs. But he made no such promises.
His only promise was to himself. Don't be a sucker.

Jeffrey was barely twenty-five when he got here. Broad
shoulders. Lean. Swift hands. Swift dick like his father. A dick
swift enough to fly him out of Barbados.

It took four months in Edmonton and two weeks in Toronto

to secure passage to New York. Beautiful though it was, staying long in Canada was not in his plans, but he'd felt obligated
to stay briefly with the woman who got him there, a pretty
blond with laughing blue eyes and fluffy marshmallow skin.
Toting a smile to match her perfect porcelain skin, she turned
up at Fisherman's Club in Dover with her policeman boyfriend
one night. In his four years as the barman at Fisherman's he'd
seen many near-perfect smiles, but hers was the real thing. She
sipped cognac; her boyfriend wolfed down rum and coke as if
it was lemonade. By closing he was drunk.

Jeffrey drove them back to their beachside condo and put
her boyfriend to bed. She was beside herself with disappointment. Seducing her that night was a stroll on the beach.

For the next week he shadowed them, showing up just
when her boyfriend was ready to slide into rum-induced
oblivion. Once the policeman was safely tucked in Jeffrey
would help his girlfriend live out her fantasy of romance
under a Caribbean moonlit sky the boyfriend has promised.
Back in Edmonton, she dumped her boyfriend, and sent
Jeffrey a plane ticket.

There was no way a woman could be more deferential to
a man. His plan was to stay three weeks, but the lifestyle she
allowed him—access to a grand condominium in town, pres-
ents and uninhibited sex—almost changed his mind. In the
end, his mother's voice restored his resolve. One Sunday
morning while his girlfriend was at church he boarded a
plane for Ontario.

He landed in Mississauga to lodge with a friend who once
worked with him at the Fisherman's. His stay there was
short. Unhappily married, his friend was not at all happy to
see him.

After two weeks of searching he found a woman who said she could get him across the border for a fee. They left after midnight and four hours later he was in Buffalo where he boarded a Greyhound bus to Manhattan.

The picture in his wallet of his daughter, Karina, was taken when she was six weeks. She was now three years old. He'd never seen her in person and this picture, with her eyes closed, was the only one he had. What did she look like today?

Each time he applied for a visa to the States he got turned down. What guarantee do we have that you will not stay in the United States, the consul officer wanted to know.

All I want to do is see my daughter.

The consular officer was unimpressed with his paternal yearning.

Karina's mother, Maria, had not returned to the island since that summer of '95. In one of her letters she declared that the only reason she didn't get an abortion was because of God. She was a good Catholic girl from Queens.

Why weren't you thinking of God when I was inside you, he wrote back.

That was the last time he heard from her until the picture came. He cursed himself for being so swift. Dick too swift. Mouth too swift.

On the corner of Forty-second and Broadway he took out his tiny black book. He leafed through sea-water-stained leaves, halting at the page with his father's Brooklyn address. Cars, trucks and buses pounded the air about him, creating a jungle of noise at decibel levels he'd never before experienced.

He stared at his father's address with surreal intensity, unmoved by the army of passersby jostling him in their hurry. Doubt bubbled in his stomach as the craziness of what he was about to do hit him. The only memory of his father was of a tall bald man leaning against a beat-up Vauxhall with a wide white woman at his side.

"That's your father over there." His mother hissed. "You see, he married a white woman so he got nuff money. Go ask him what he bring back from America for yuh?"

He was nine. His father, who'd been a myth up until then, had brought nothing. Only harsh words.

Who tell you I is you father? Tell that woman I say she lie. You ain't look nutten like me.

Was the Brooklyn address for the man his mother called Jockey correct? He'd gotten it from his cousin, who'd gotten it from her grandmother, his father's aunt.

With the help of the African cab driver he found the house on East Forty-seventh Street. He thanked the driver and stepped backward on the sidewalk to watch the yellow car drive off. His stomach suddenly felt hollow, as if some evil spirit had invaded his body and scooped out his intestines. The flat gray sky seemed to rise and drift off like a heavy balloon.

What if it was the wrong address? What if Jockey denied him as he did that time back in Barbados? Like water on his brain, those words uttered by his father some 16 years ago still floated in Jeffrey's head. Where would he go? Where would he sleep?

Contrary to his friend Nails' opinion, this trip was not about his father. Nothing there to claim. Too late to make up for the pain. All he hoped for was a spot of kindness from the man. A place to sleep for a while, until he got his stake in the ground. He didn't expect love. Love had always been a luxury to Jeffrey. He'd never been capable of following love's narrow path. But his mother never let him forget who his father was.

You look just like your father. Don't let nobody fool you, Jockey is you father.

Slowly he started up the steps with his suitcase, which contained a few pieces of clothing, three pairs of shoes and his CDs. Music was the liquid in which he bathed his soul, trying to drown the nightmare of growing up poor. He never went anywhere without his music.

He rapped the door and waited. Presently a tall bald man with a thin gray mustache peeped through Venetian blinds at an unwashed window.

"Yes?"

"Jockey?"

"Who want to know?"

"Jeffrey. Your son."

The long pause brimmed with confusion and deliberation. Jeffrey breathed deeply the heavy November air, and strained to hear the other man's thoughts.

The man left the window; then the front door opened slightly.

"You coming in?"

Jeffrey knuckled his way through the crack between the doorjamb and the gaunt man.

"You get tall, boy," the man whispered.

Now standing in a dim hallway opposite his father, Jeffrey wanted to say. *I'm twenty-five. Hardly a boy.* Instead he grinned nervously and said, "Tall like you."

Jockey grunted and closed the door. "Come in and sit down. You want a drink? I got some Bacardi rum. It ain't Mount Gay, but it gets the job done."

"No thanks. I don't drink," he lied.

"You don't drink? What kind of man are you? Boy, you ain't my son if you don't drink."

"I don't care about being your son. I just want a place to stay for a little while."

Curtly spoken and laced with anger these words were born sixteen years ago and had been laying in the grass of his shame, coiled, aged, ready to strike.

The older man swayed like a palm tree in a high wind, then shrugged and crawled back into his aloof skin, drawing his lips tight around him. His eyes closed briefly as though he was about to fall asleep on his feet. Then he stumbled backward.

Jeffrey, already beginning to curse his swiftness, realized the man was drunk. "I'm sorry."

His father fell into a chair and sat in a straightjacket staring dead ahead. The sultry silence blew up a storm of soul-searching for memories that didn't exist.

Jeffrey picked up his suitcase.

"You can stay. Stay as long as you want. It's a big house. Three bedrooms and a finished basement. Nobody in it but me. Gets lonely as hell sometimes."

"I don't expect to be here long."

"Look, boy, I know you must be angry with me. I wish things was different. But them ain't. I wish we had some memories to joke about. If that's what you come up here for."

"I ain't come up here for you," Jeffrey blurted.

Jockey twisted around to face him. "What you come up here for if you ain't come looking for the past?"

"I looking for the future. I here to find my daughter."

"You got a daughter?"

"Three years old."

"You got any pictures?"

Jeffrey scooped the tattered picture from his wallet. He handed it to his father and saw the man's body relax, saw a sudden transformation in his face; the eyes suddenly opening wide enough to engulf an eclipse, his smile exploding into a grin.

"White woman?"

Jeffrey nodded.

"You like them white women?"

Jeffrey wondered if his father was trying to make fun of him. "They like me."

"Yeah, I think I know why."

"It ain't what you thinking."

His father chuckled. "What I thinking?"

"It ain't what you thinking."

maria had written three letters. In the first letter she loved and missed him and wished she could've stayed longer on the island. By the next letter she had found out she was pregnant and cursed him for being so careless. That was when she declared herself too good a Catholic to have an abortion. She did not respond to his letter until nine months later. That last letter contained a picture with the baby's name and birth weight on the back. His first week in New York he tried calling the telephone number she'd given him, but nobody ever seemed to be home.

it irked him every time his father posed as the interested grandfather.

"Where this grandchild of mine?"

Why didn't you ask for me like this, he wanted to reply. Instead he would feign temporary deafness.

Fifteen years divorced, his father never remarried and had no other children. From the look of things he received a decent pension from his retired post office job. The untidy house sat in the middle of a well-kept block in a neighborhood of single and two-family homes mostly owned by West Indians. The expanse and energy of the city thrilled Jeffrey and he tried to ignore his father slovenliness while trying to figure out a way to find his daughter.

New York's well-publicized reputation for violence and crime didn't intimidate him. In his mind he was born for the big city. It didn't take him long to find the West Indian clubs. The Cave on Rutland Road was one such joint. There he ran into Tallabo, someone he knew casually from the nightclub scene back home.

He'd first seen Maria in Tallabo's company at the club where he worked, and concluded that she was much too pretty for him. Being the bartender, it was easy to strike up a conversation with Maria and before the night was over he had all the information he needed: where she was staying and her room and telephone number. The rest was easy. Tallabo didn't have his looks, his style, didn't have a job and didn't have a car. He picked Maria up the next day in his Honda and took her on a tour of the island. That night they ran into Tallabo in a club. After a juvenile attempt to intimidate him Tallabo accepted that he'd lost Maria and took up with her traveling companion.

Over rum punch in the Cave they joked about the *life.*

"Them was some nice days," said Tallabo. "Them tourist women was some freaky bitches."

"Remember that short fat chick you picked up at Golden Sands? She was traveling with a dark-haired fire-in-her-eyes beauty name Maria."

"Yeah, the Maria you tried to steal from me."

Jeffrey laughed. "Tried? Boy, you memory bad."

Tallabo smirked. "Nobody like you could ever steal a woman from me."

"Let we leave that alone for now. I wanna know about the other girl.What was her name again?"

"Samantha Seltzer."

"You ever tried to contact her when you got up here?"

Tallabo was a big dude, broad of shoulder with a square ridge for a forehead. He traced a circle on his forehead with his fingers and cracked a block of ice in his mouth. His eyes flickered like damp fires. "Why would I wanna do that?"

"You got her number? I wanna call her."

"No. And if I did I wouldn't give it to you."

"Jeez, man, you ain't gotta be like that."

"Like what? Everything cool."

When he got home he called information and got numbers for S. A. Seltzer in Brooklyn and Samantha Seltzer in Queens. He called both numbers. Neither party was home and he left his number.

The next day Samantha called. She seemed genuinely excited to hear him. Riding this wave of good fortune he asked about Maria.

"There's something you should know about Maria."

"What," he asked. There was a long pause. "What's the problem? She dead or something."

"I don't want to talk about it on the phone. Would you like to get together for a drink tomorrow night?"

his father found him in bed the next afternoon reading Sports Illustrated and smoking a Winston.

"Wanna go around the corner and have a drink with me?"

He looked up from the magazine. The man's eyes were crimson. How did he see? The dingy blue T-shirt he was wearing seemed too small and was frayed at the neck. The armpits were dark with sweat stains. Jeffrey took a deep drag on his cigarette, flicked ash in the tray on the floor.

"I can't. Going out later." He flipped the page of the magazine and exhaled slowly, trying to delay having to breathe the sour fermented smell of sweat and alcohol released by his father.

"When you going to bring that granddaughter of mine to meet her grandfather?"

"How many times I gotta say I ain't find her yet?" He closed the magazine and got up to dump the contents of the ashtray into the garbage bucket in the kitchen.

"You ain't find her? What you mean you ain't find her?" His father trailed behind, just off his left shoulder.

"Jeffrey spun sharply. "That's what I mean. I ain't find her."

"Maybe you ashamed to bring her here to meet me. Is that it?"

Jeffrey stepped around Jockey and sauntered back to the bedroom with his father at his heels like a faithful puppy.

"I wasn't always like this, you know," murmured Jockey. "Before I get fire from my job."

"I thought you say you retire?"

"I was forced to retire. To me it's the same shit. If you black they think they can do anything to you."

"Who's *they*?"

"Don't play stupid, boy. Who you think run this fucking country?"

"Look, I ain't really wanna hear this."

Jeffrey picked up a pair of jeans from the floor by the bed and started to get dressed. He hadn't expected love to blossom between them, but he'd hoped they would get along. The man's bitterness and his perpetual drunken state made it impossible to entertain any emotion but pity. He couldn't even hate him. He pulled on his boots, took a shirt from the rack in the closet and grabbed a brown leather bomber hanging on the bedroom door.

"I ain't finish with you yet," said Jockey.

"Save it for your drinking buddies around the corner. I got places to go."

"Wake up, boy. You better off forgetting 'bout that child."

"Like you did me."

"I left your ass back there because your mother was a whore. I wasn't the only man swimming in that ocean."

Jeffrey's reaction was swift. Too swift. The right hook landed flush on Jockey's jaw. The man sagged to the floor. Jeffrey swung the flimsy wooden door open and went out into the clear evening.

he rode the number 2 train to Brooklyn Heights and walked to the promenade. Sitting on one of the green benches he watched the setting sun tore the sky to shreds and cursed his swiftness.

Mouth too swift.

Hands too swift.

Like it or not the man is your father. Striking your father is against God's law.

Feeling sorrow canoeing in his chest he got up to go apologize to his father. Then he sat down again. Perhaps it was better to wait. His father might not be too forgiving right now. He'd take a bottle of rum home later and work up to it over a drink.

He cursed himself double for showing his mother Karina's picture. He could still hear her admonishment: *Boy you going let that little girl grow up and not know her father? You going to be just like your father Jockey?"*

samantha lived in Park Slope. He arrived early and sat on the sofa while she set her face. They took a cab to Banana Boat, a cozy tropical theme bar on Flatbush Avenue where the drinks were mixed to taste.

Sitting at the bar he ordered two piña coladas.

"Remember the piña coladas I mixed for you at Fisherman's Club?"

She laughed. "How could I forget? Got me in big trouble. That was the last night I wore panties on the island. I know you don't believe me but all I came down there for was to get some rest. I wasn't looking for sex."

Jeffrey sipped from the large glass. "I believe you."

"No you don't. Not with that devilish grin on your face. After those piña coladas the word *no* had lost all meaning. And the truth is I would've rather said yes to you."

He smiled. Samantha was a large woman, not really his type. Her round blue eyes sparkled too brightly to be natural. She had short frizzy blond hair still showing black roots. But her large sensuous mouth always hinting of laughter was proving seductive. Perhaps. It'd been a while since he had some.

"Do I look the same?" she asked.

"Better?"

"You're just saying that. When we met you didn't look my way twice."

He laughed. "You had your eyes on somebody else."

"No, I had my eyes on you, but your cock was already hard for Maria."

He laughed nervously. "What's the story with Maria?"

She sighed. "I don't know where to begin."

"Begin with where she living."

Samantha touched his right triceps and let her fingers linger, caressing them suggestively. "Look, Maria was only nineteen when she got pregnant. The pregnancy was very hard on her. And her strict family didn't help. They practically disowned her. The poor girl had a nervous breakdown. I don't know what you did to her in those three weeks but she claimed she loved you."

"I want to see her."

"You're too late."

"What about the baby?"

"Karina?"

"Yes. Karina is my child."

A voice boomed behind him. "Why don't you shut your blasted mouth telling people Karina is your child?"

Jeffrey turned slowly. Tallabo stood over his right shoulder, sullen as a Voodoo priest.

"This ain't got nothing to do with you, fool," Jeffrey said.

Samantha tightened her grip on his arm to calm him down.

Jeffrey breathed deep and sighed. He stood up to take his wallet out. "Let's get out of here."

"Who the hell you calling a fool?" Tallabo growled.

"What's your problem, man?"

"You're my problem. You need to get Karina off your damn mind."

"Don't do this here," Samantha said."

You shoulda stayed where you were," Tallabo said.

Jeffrey put ten dollars on the bar. "Maybe you're the one shoulda stayed back there. Acting all backward like an idiot. Karina is my daughter."

"Maria is my wife. And Karina is my daughter."

The words banged off Jeffrey's head, then floated back, hovering around before trickling into his mind slowly like syrup.

He looked at Samantha. "What's this fool talking about?"

She bowed her head and rimmed her drink with her pinkie.

He turned back to Tallabo. "You're talking gibberish. Maria would never marry a monkey like you. Go get a towel and wipe the drool from your mouth."

The shove Tallabo gave Jeffrey wasn't even hard enough to make him rock on his heels. But Jeffrey's reaction was swift. A hard straight right to Tallaboo's face. The man flopped to the floor.

Taking Samantha by the arm, Jeffrey started for the door. He didn't expect Tallabo to get up. Not after taking his best punch.

No one had time to warn him. Perhaps no one wanted to. In an instant the knife Tallabo wielded was buried in his back.

Jeffrey stumbled outside. It was raining. People rushing past, hoping to disappear before the police arrived. Samantha screaming. He wanted to tell her to stop screaming; that her voice was hurting his ears, but his mouth wouldn't open. His equilibrium was disappearing fast. For a moment his father stood in front of him. And then vanished. Jeffrey took a step then he fell, his head resting gently against an empty St. Ives bottle; ten inches of steel rising from his back like a silver obelisk. A face flashed before him. Maria? Or was that Karina's face? He'd come all this way just to see that face. She looked so much like her mother. Mouth set the same way. The streetlight charged the silver strip on the bottle's edge, sending a crackle of light bouncing off his wet cheek. How quickly does a body go cold when blood runs to water on a rainy street?

"ssshhhh! ssshhhh! Don't try to talk."

Jeffrey opened his eyes a crack. Was this Heaven? It felt awfully cold in Heaven. Everything was hazy.

"You gonna make it, son," a voice said.

Make it? He thought he was already there.

He had no feeling in any part of his body.

"You gonna be alright, son. You gonna be alright. You lost a lot of blood. It was touch and go. But you gonna be alright."

It sounded like his father.

"Yeah, we gonna be alright. You and me. You lost a lot of blood. And won't you know, your blood type is one of the rarest. They couldn't find it in the hospital. But guess what? We's the same blood type. Ain't that something. Yeah. Me and you. Rare, but a perfect match.

"You know, I really didn't mean that stuff I said about your mother. I know you don't wanna hear it now. After all, you got your own troubles, but I was feeling real bitter. But when they bring me to the hospital and tell me that you might die if you didn't get blood, well... I got scared. I didn't want you to die. And then they found out we had the same blood. It is a miracle. It is a miracle that you living, boy. And then it come to me that the Lord keep me around for this purpose. That this was my purpose. You know how many times I wanted to check out? With all the shite that has happened to me, this was God's way of saying that my life still mean something. I have to tell you, son, I feel better today than I ever feel in my life. I never give you nothing as a child. But I get a chance to give you a second life. I called your mother and tell her you alright. That I will be bringing you home soon. I ain't got nothing to keep me here."

baseball lifted his head from the couch and waited for his owl eyes to adjust to the darkness. Eyelids as heavy as the drawn green damask blinds at the window. From the sounds outside he knew it was still daylight. Night or day. Didn't make much difference to him now.

So tired. Too freaking tired to move. But he was hungry. Hadn't eaten all day. Going on three days now without sleep. Every time he closed his eyes, the sharp echo of a barking gun kept ringing in his head. And then he would hear wooden laughter; somebody mocking him. Didn't have to think to hard to figure who that somebody could be. He sat up and flexed his arms, feeling his power swell. He missed working out. But right now the weight of being alone was a Mack truck on his chest. He was a bat dreading daylight, and it made him angry.

Wish I had a woman up in this mutha, he thought, getting up to turn the TV on.

The large two-bedroom apartment belonged to an old, chain-smoking Puerto Rican dude, named Rico, who once worked with his grandmother. Rico suffered with emphysema and had been on disability for years. From time to time, at the request of his grandmother, Baseball delivered clothes and food to Rico. About a month ago, Rico went into the hospital and hadn't come out yet. Impressed by Baseball's kind soul (Rico's words) he gave Baseball keys to the apartment and asked him to drop by once in a while to water his plants. The apartment was a mess. Baseball cleaned it up. It was now his only secure hideaway.

But for how long? It was only a matter of time before the police or Phisto found out about this crib.

He became absorbed in a show about horses on one of those nature channels. Two horses pranced around, touching noses in a courtship dance. Then the slender stallion sprawled on top of the black mare, which did what most of the women he knew would do: she whinnied and backed away.

He'd always loved horses. Rode one a long time ago and fell in love. Well, okay, that wasn't a real horse. It was a pony at one of those street fairs which came to Prospect Park in the summer. But it was his dream to own a house one day on a large plot of land with enough open space for horses.

Working for Phisto was supposed to be his ticket to the good life. Big home. Money. Cars. Horses. Phisto even promised that he would one day be able to own his own private plane. Imagine that. Like a movie star, flying around with your own fucking wings. He'd name the plane Baseball. What else?

But it hadn't turned out that way. The way Phisto said it would. He could've had a different life, that's what made him crazy now that he realized his days were numbered.

He used to have other plans. That was before Phisto came along. His hard-working Bajan grandmother raised him after his mother got married and moved to Alaska when he was seven. She took education seriously and made sure he did too, never letting him out to play before he'd done his school-work. He was a good enough student. "B's" and "C's" mostly. The occasional "A" would have his grandmother beaming. But dancing had been his real passion.

His grandmother wanted him to go to college. And he did so just to please her. Nobody can say he didn't give it a shot. Two years of computer science classes at Iona. But that was before Phisto came along flashing a roll of Benjamins in his face. Before Phisto mesmerized him with the offer of easy money and hyper-sexed women. Had he stayed at Iona and gotten his degree who knew where he'd be today. Maybe on Wall Street writing programs to analyze the stock market. Maybe writing new game applications for Xbox. Instead, he was facing death on the streets.

Rico had stocked up enough canned food to weather an apocalypse. By day 3, Baseball was sick of canned tuna and had eaten so much baked beans he was farting beans in his sleep. And the Campbell's beef soup: after five days that shit looked like vomit. Tonight he was in the mood for a hamburger. Yeah. A big juicy Mickey D's.

Shortly after midnight he stepped outside for the first time in six days. He'd taken precaution to ditch his usual street heat—baggy pants and oversized T-shirt—for a disguise. In the old man's closet he found a blue double-breasted suit.

Was a size too big, but that was OK. The white shirt was also too large. Hardly noticeable underneath the suit. A blue and yellow striped tie completed his costume. The man looking back at him in the mirror shocked him. Damn! He looked like a Fortune 500 CEO or something.

Calm for a Friday night in Brooklyn. Hardly anybody on the street at all. Where're all the freaks? May was one of those months in New York where the weather could change on a dime. But it was warm. And warm nights brought the crazies dancing in the streets. Then he remembered it was the first of the month. Welfare checks would've been cashed. The freaks would've copped their sacks and gone underground to stew.

Six blocks to the MacDonald's on Knickerbocker. He felt like a new person in his new clothes. Probably better odds of having a heart attack than of anyone from Phisto's crew recognizing him in this costume, still, he couldn't afford to be complacent. No matter how he dressed, he was still a wanted man and one mistake could mean his life.

Two weeks ago somebody tried to kill him. As he was coming out of his house in Flatbush a car pulled up and one of the bangers opened fire. Baseball was lucky the dude was a bad shot.

Had to have been on Phisto's order. Baseball was certain because he was half expecting it. After what he witnessed in the park, and after his reaction, Baseball knew exactly how Phisto would respond.

A case of being in the wrong place at the wrong time. He wasn't even supposed to be there the night Phisto shot Dupree in Lincoln Terrace Park. That night he was supposed to be watching Alvin Ailey at City Center.

This young Jamaican chick he'd met online had invited him to the dance concert. As a student at the Ailey school she got discounted tickets. He was so excited. For the first time he confided in someone his regret about not following his heart and auditioning for LaGuardia High School when he had the chance. Instead, he went to Brooklyn Tech, a choice that gave his grandmother more joy and satisfaction than it did him.

He was already dressed and ready to go when Rosalie called and cancelled. Bad shrimp cocktail at a party the night before. Whatever.

Baseball was standing no more than a foot away from Dupree when Phisto shot him in the head. One minute they were joking around. Next minute: Boom!

First time he'd witnessed a shooting. Dupree's blood splattered all over Baseball's leather jacket. Seeing his jacket decorated with Dupree's blood and brains caused Baseball to heave immediately. Phisto thought it was so funny and called him a pussy.

Baseball threw the jacket in the garbage. Phisto made him retrieve it and ordered him to go home and burn the shit. Who could've predicted what transpired next.

Undone by shock, Baseball drove so erratically that the police pulled him over on Linden Boulevard. He jumped from the car and ran, leaving the jacket behind.

Phisto did not tolerate snitches. Was the very reason Dupree was made dead. After Baseball's pathetic performance in the park Phisto would see him as a weak link, unable to hold up under police pressure. In Phisto's world that equaled dead.

Baseball tried to push those thoughts from his mind. A nice juicy burger would give him the fuel to figure out what was what.

At Madison, he passed a couple walking their dog. The woman looked at him and he saw suspicion in her eyes. Damn. Even when you wear a suit, a black man ain't free of suspicious glances on the street. Even from his own people. Ain't that some shit! He wanted to laugh, but knew the shit wasn't funny.

A young girl at a bus stop eyed him, almost respectfully, as he crossed Cornelia. She smiled and said something, which he didn't hear. Didn't really wanna hear. Probably a prostitute. She was pretty, though. She called after him, calling him 'Daddy', but he ignored her and turned onto Jefferson. McDonald's was at the end of the block.

He liked this Mickey D's because it stayed open late. He'd worked there one summer when he was in high school. Pay was 6.50 an hour then. Heard it wasn't much better now. Worked out good for him in the end. Met Monique James there for one. She was a heavy-set girl who lived down the block from the Methodist church. Monique was the best piece of ass he's ever had. Still thought so to this day. Forget the Karma sutra or whatever that book was called. Things that girl did with his willy could not be found in any manual or any movie.

Heard she'd gotten married to a minister from Philadelphia and had moved there to raise her family. Wished he could have her tonight.

He circled the block once before going inside, checking the parking lot for familiar whips. Phisto was quite fond of McDonald's himself. It wouldn't be out of character for him to drop into the nearest golden arch for a late-night snack.

There were only three cars Phisto would be caught dead in. A black Escalade with 40s, a black Mercedes and a black BMW 7-series; all of them tricked out like James Bond's Alfa-Romeo with recording equipment, cameras and hidden compartments, all of which Baseball had installed. That'd been his job with Phisto for the past two years. Personal driver and electronics guru. Kept Baseball rolling in cheddar without having to sling on the street corner.

None of the cars in the lot were familiar. Still, he checked to make sure his gun was secure in his waistband before pushing the yellow doors open.

Bright as day inside. There were only two people on duty. A pimpled-face youngster with cornrows and a hunched-over woman whose elaborately braided hair was tinged with gray. Her expression reminded him of somebody being strangled. From the way she was stooped over with a futile, weary look in her eyes, he figured she had a bad back or arthritis or something. Another glance at the woman's devitalized body and he knew why her presence disturbed him.

She reminded him of his late cousin. He could tell that she was younger than she looked. The premature graying of her hair mocked the firm skin around her eyes. He'd seen it before. His cousin had turned gray by the time she was twenty-five and suffered from diabetes, high-blood pressure and arthritis before she got to thirty. She died at thirty-five, a victim of the pain and disease. The doctor said she ate too much fast-food, but he didn't buy that shit. He believed she'd been poisoned.

"Can I help you?" the young attendant said.

"Double cheese with fries."

"Anything to drink."

"Coke. Super size."

He paid for his order and leaned on the counter, staring at the color-coded menu, at the way the colors almost inspired you to order one of everything on the menu. It was the middle of the night but looking at the list he was almost stirred to order a McMuffin to go with his cheeseburger.

He watched the woman struggle to scoop fries from the bin. She gripped the ladle with difficulty, her fingers unable to close around the handle. He wanted to tell the young man to go over and help her, but kept quiet. People like her were usually full of pride.

As he walked out of the restaurant with his food he remembered how hard it was to watch his cousin struggle with day to day business, like tying her sneakers. Things he'd taken for granted, things she'd taught him to do when he was a kid.

He shook his head and stuffed several fries into him mouth. Damn. The shit was good. His mind flew back to the tender at the bus stop. Maybe he'd see what she was up to now that he'd fed his fix.

She was in the same spot, leaning against the bus stop, her knapsack over her shoulder, her short denim skirt now higher up her leg. She looked clean and had a strong face. The light from the street lamp surrounded her with a quiet glow.

"You waiting for the bus?" He mumbled though a mouthful of fries.

She smiled. "You shouldn't eat that stuff. Especially so late."

"What stuff?"

She pointed at the McDonald's bag.

"This? What's wrong with it?"

"Where you live?" she said.

"Around the way. How about you?"

"Far away."

"What you doing over here?"

"I took a walk."

He laughed. "You took a walk and ended up here?"

"Yeah."

"How far did you walk?"

"I don't know. A lot."

"You must be tired."

"Yes. I couldn't walk any more so I decided to wait for the bus."

"So where exactly is far away?"

"The Bronx."

"The Bronx?" He moved closer. "The Bronx? What time you gonna get home?"

With a resigned shoulder shrug she yielded space, backing up a few paces. "Whenever I get home."

"Bus don't run very often this time of night," he said.

"I know that too." She shifted her weight. "So?"

"So?"

"What you wanna do?"

"About what?"

"This situation."

He gazed at her, thinking. He knew what she was saying, but he had to be careful. She could be anybody and right now anybody could be the wrong person to be with.

He stuffed a handful of fries into his mouth. "I don't know."

"You live alone?"

"Yeah, I got my own crib and shit. Nothing big, yunno. It's clean though. I keep it clean."

"You wanna take me back to your crib?"

"I don't know."

"Look. . . ."

He looked into her eyes and saw fear. She really didn't seem like the kind of girl who should be out here on the streets.

"How much?" He asked.

"For what?"

"Whatever. . . You know."

She shrugged. "How much you wanna pay?"

"How much you worth?"

Her laugh frightened him. For someone in her circumstances it seemed to have no boundary, surging at him like a runaway horse, filling up the quiet night with its piercing pitch.

"What's your name," he asked.

"Welcome."

"Welcome. . . Hmm. Welcome what?"

"Welcome Soljean."

"Let's go, Welcome," he said.

She fell instep beside him, maneuvering the huge cracks in the uneven sidewalk with deft insider skill.

He offered her fries but she refused.

"You ain't no hooker, are you?" he said.

She did not respond and he let it go at that.

"I don't really have much at my crib to eat. A few eggs. Unless you like crackers and tuna fish."

"I'm not hungry."

He stopped and looked at her. "You sure you don't want some fries? These shits are good."

"I'm sure. Thanks."

They walked on in silence, past an empty lot where someone had tried to grow tomato trees. Mangy grass had strangled the now limp brown vines which had never borne any tomatoes. Next to that, another empty lot crammed with the ruins of old cars, discarded refrigerators and other appliances, and heaps of garbage.

He saw a black Ford Explorer approaching slowly. It stopped in the middle of the block. His first instinct was to turn and run, but he quickly realized that if Phisto was in that SUV the last thing he wanted was to confirm any suspicion they might have that this man in the suit walking toward them had reason to be afraid.

He kept his sway going, putting his arm around Welcome and smiling into her eyes. She laughed as he stopped to kiss her under a rotting oak. He leaned into her, trying too hard to overpower her with the kiss. It was fake. She probably knew it was fake too, but played along with him, sliding her hand around his neck and drawing him even closer.

They strolled past the truck. With his arm still around her waist, he stole a glance left, into the big body. Two people inside: a man and a woman with dreadlocks. Nobody he recognized.

When they reached his apartment building he scoped the street and the adjacent park quickly to make sure nobody had them under watch, then he stuck the key into the lock and twisted. The heavy iron door groaned and the building belched stale fried chicken odor as he let Welcome inside first. One last visual sweep of the street before he followed her into the lobby.

he watched her as she looked around the apartment with awe. Made him wonder where the hell she lived. The apartment wasn't all that for damn sure. Not for her to be eyeballing the crib like it was a palace. The old man had stocked it with pretty nice furniture. The brown leather sofa was a touch of class. He wouldn't have bought that gray grand-father recliner himself; it didn't compliment anything else in the room, but it was comfy.

"Why don't you put your bag down?" he said.

She stood without moving and he got the impression she hadn't even heard him. He walked over to take the bag off her back. She flinched and retreated a few steps. Their eyes locked. In her wide brown eyes, he saw with clarity the mark of despair.

"I'm sorry," she said.

"I was just gonna take your bag. It looks heavy."

"Yeah, it is. Thanks."

She bent forward so he could remove the bulging knapsack from her slender back. He could almost make out the ridges of her shoulder blade in the thin cotton shirt.

"Damn, you weren't kidding. Shit's heavy as a dead man," he said. "What's in here?"

"Books," she said.

"Books? Just books?"

She nodded. "My school books."

"Your school books?"

She nodded again. "And some clothes."

He waited for her to explain and when she didn't he figured he'd better get some ticklish matters out of the way. "How old are you?"

"Seventeen."

"You sure?"

"What difference does it make? I'm here."

"Yeah, you're here. That's true."

Her sad eyes focused on his face. "If I do it, can I stay the night?"

"If you do what?"

"You know. . ." She averted her gaze. Her eyes fell on the picture on the wall. "Is that your father?"

"No."

"Who is he?"

"Just somebody," he replied. "What's your name?"

She giggled softly. "I told you my name."

"Oh, yeah. I'm losing it. Welcome, right?"

She nodded. "What's yours?"

"Rae-Qwon. Call me Baseball."

"Is that what everybody calls you?"

"Yeah."

She looked him in the eye for the first time. "I want to call you something else."

"Something else?"

"Yeah."

"Why?"

She shrugged. "I don't know. Just wanna."

"What you wanna call me?"

"Ray."

"Ray?"

"Yeah. . . Ray."

"Nobody calls me Ray."

"Then I'm gonna call you Ray."

He felt a big smile coming on and put his hands over his mouth. Why did it feel so good that she wanted to call him Ray?

"So, Ray, can I. . . Stay the night if we do it?"

"Sure," he replied.

There were many things he wanted to ask her, but he wasn't sure there was any point to it. All she wanted was a place to sleep, that much was clear to him. Which meant that she probably got kicked out of her home or she lived in some roach-infested shelter with no privacy where drug addicts and women running from domestic violence took out their anger and frustration on each other.

He opened the McDonald bag in his hand and stuck his hand inside. The fries were already cold.

"You must be tired," he said.

She shrugged and drew her arms tightly around her body as if she was cold.

He looked at her and knew he wasn't going to touch that booty tonight. She was cute, though. A little on the skinny side, but hey.

He said, "You wanna take a shower?"

"That would be nice."

"It's down the hall to the right. There's towels in the closet outside the bathroom."

She got halfway down the hall before she turned around. "I'm a virgin, you know."

"You're a virgin?"

"Yes. I want to stay a virgin until I get married. Is that okay?"

"What do you mean?"

"I can't do it the regular way."

He bowed his head and put a hand to his mouth to redirect the gas he felt churning in his chest. He burped loudly and smelled tuna fish on his breath. Welcome's face broke out in a big smile. He was still trying to figure out what the hell she meant.

"You can't do it the regular way?"

"No. . . But, it's cool the other way. The back way." She paused. "If you want. A lotta boys like to do it that way."

"You mean. . ."

"Yes."

"I've never done it that way," he said.

It was a lie, but the truth was he didn't really like doing it. He'd seen it done in many of the porn movies he'd watched and tried it with the preacher's daughter. Didn't take him long to figure out that it wasn't his flow.

She smiled as if she knew he was lying. "I don't mind, really."

"We'll talk about it later." It was all he could think to say.

he took her bag into the bedroom. For a while he sat on the bed staring rigidly at the blank wall. He still had the Mickey D's bag in his hand, with the unwrapped cheese-burger inside. His appetite was gone. Didn't know what it was but this girl moved him. There was something uncommon about her, which made him think hard about what it would mean to go through with their bargain.

Was it because she made no attempt to mask the pain of her life? It was clear in her eyes, there for all to see. But, again, that wasn't all you saw when you looked at her. A quiet determination also burned in those eyes. She was going places, that one. He'd only just met her, but found himself hoping he'd be around to see it.

He smiled at the thought and opened the Mickey D's bag. The smell of hot cheese and beef was suddenly more than his stomach could assimilate. He dropped the bag and ran from the room. The bathroom door was closed but not locked. He pushed it and rushed inside. She was sitting on the toilet. Before he could stop himself he puked all over her legs.

his hands trembled as he unbuttoned her pale blue blouse. It felt like silk, but it wasn't. No doubt she bought it on sale at some discount store.

She noticed his hands shaking and stopped him. With delicate-boned fingers she proceeded to do it herself, taking her bra off too, cupping her perky breasts in her small hands. They were just the right size; not large, but not small either. Her extremely large nipples were surrounded by very dark irregular-shaped aureoles. She cupped her breasts, lifting them for his gaze, offering them to him.

His mind flew back to all those pornos he'd watched in his uncle's basement when he was barely sixteen. None of the women had breasts like these.

He leaned forward and kissed them. Each one. Slowly. Gently. Nibbling the nipples' edge, trying to hold off the urge to attack them, to attach himself to them with the hungry desperation of a child.

He wondered if she sensed that he needed her more than she needed him. Did he even want to have sex? He wasn't sure. More than anything he wanted to be reassured that he would wake up to see the next day.

He kissed her wet mouth, overpowering her with his pent up fear. His neediness. His desperation. He could feel her smiling under his kiss. As if she knew he was feeding her his fear and gladly accepted it.

Her kisses became more passionate as his intensity swelled. Time flowed. Juices accumulated. He'd never kissed anyone this much and this long. But he liked it. The slow passing of time as their kisses became deeper and more frantic. He didn't want to stop kissing her, even as she began undressing him.

Pants.

Shirt.

Undershirt.

Boxers.

Completely naked, he lay back on the couch. She was touching every part of his body and seemed to be doing it all at once. As if she had more than two hands.

No way she's seventeen. No way.

He felt himself floating in space. The kind of feeling he got after he smoked a wooler. But he wasn't high. At least not on any narcotic. Hadn't smoked a joint in a week. There was no part of his body she didn't touch. He gasped every time she bit his leg. Every tongue-glide over his hips.

No way she's seventeen. No way.

He tried to sit up. She forced him back down and got on her knees on the couch, taking hold of his very hard penis and began to rub it firmly. She moved effortlessly forward until her mouth was near it, breathing dragon-hot breath onto the tip. Eagerly, she stretched out her tongue to salt the head.

Baseball felt his body slowly swaying like a pendulum, but he was unaware of starting the motion or even controlling it.

He was hearing a sound, a music in his head, put there by the rhythm of Welcome's breathing, the circular rhythm of her lips dancing around his hardness.

As he neared explosion, she released him and leaned back on the couch, with her beautiful breasts pointing majestically upward and said, "Come on my breast."

The orgasm was so intense that he almost broke down and cried. He fell limp next to her on the couch, exhausted, and contented.

"No way, you're seventeen. No way. You gotta be at least twenty."

She smiled and caressed his left earlobe.

He began to doze off. It was going to be hard sending her away in the morning.

he made the call from a pay phone half expecting his grandmother not to pick up. She was happy to hear him and cried throughout the conversation. Ever since her sweet bread-baking Bajan husband had run back to Barbados after a robbery at the bank where he worked as a guard his grandmother had been threatening to return home herself. That was 20 years ago. Baseball was too young to remember meeting him, but any man who would run and leave his wife was a punk. Growing up he heard all about the man's famous sweetbread from his grandmother. Sweetbread or not he was still a punk.

But now, it appeared that she was going to make good on her threat. She was fed up with America, and what Baseball had done with his life. After she told him about the police coming to visit her again, his grandmother told him she had put the house up for sale and was packing to leave for Barbados.

His mind began flipping through scenarios where he was caught by police and forced to snitch on Phisto. If he hadn't fully comprehended it before, reality butted him between the eyes now. He was a dead man. Who was he kidding. He needed to be gone from New York.

He walked back to the apartment furiously orchestrating the next few hours in his head. Saying goodbye to Welcome would be difficult. A remarkable concession to someone who'd been in his life for just a few hours.

she'd cooked eggs for breakfast. How was she to know that he was allergic to them? Her even thinking about cooking him a meal only added to her bewitching effect on him. She was so apologetic, he had to leave the room for a while to avoid laughing and possibly hurting her feelings.

He prepared his beans and they ate together at the tiny kitchen table. The kitchen smelled of garlic and basil which she had mixed with her eggs. Garlic was good for the blood, she kept telling him. But he hated the smell.

He looked at her and saw her pupils dancing in the light coming in through the window. He'd forgotten to tell her not to open the curtains. The sunlight felt good though. It made the kitchen bright and the green cupboards, which he thought before were ugly, seemed almost beautiful in the sunlight.

Beneath the table her toes traced circles on his ankle. He smiled and the idea of making love to her on the kitchen floor made him kiddy.

"Do you wanna talk about it?" she said.

"Talk about what?"

"Whatever's bothering you," she replied.

He tried to laugh. "Nothing's bothering me. You're making me horny playing with my foot like that. That's what's bothering me."

"Where did you go when you went out this morning?"

His voice got testy. "I went for a walk."

"I'm sorry. Am I being too nosy?"

"I went to get some fresh air, that's all. No big deal."

"You looked frightened when you came back. You looked like something's on your mind."

He could feel his brow tighten. She'd tripped the fuse of his anxiety. Rage was beginning to brew. He got up and walked to the window. He knew he shouldn't be standing at the window, but he had to bring his anger under control or he might just heave it all at her. That wouldn't be right.

He turned around. "Have you called your mother?"

"Yes."

"Liar."

"Well. . . I didn't call her directly. She doesn't have a phone. But I called my grandmother. My mother goes to visit her every day. I told her to tell my mother I'm staying with a friend and not to worry."

"Did you leave this number?"

"Yes." She paused. "Is that ok?"

"I suppose."

"Who're you running from, Ray?"

His stare was as blank as the wall. He couldn't answer her. Not truthfully anyway.

"I could get birth control, you know," she offered. "I could go on the pill. Or get the patch."

"Birth control?"

"Yeah. . . You know."

"I thought you wanted to save yourself."

"Yeah. But what am I saving it for anyway? I mean. . . Men don't save themselves, so why should a woman?"

"You plan on going to college?"

"Yeah. I gotta go. I want to get a scholarship for college. I need to. If not I can't go. But I'm not sure if I can get a good enough score on the SATs to make it. But I have to go to college."

"Yeah. You should go to college."

"Did you go?"

He hesitated. "Yeah."

"Where?"

"Iona."

"You graduated?"

"No."

"I wanna be a doctor. I can't end up like my mother and my friends. I can't be poor. I don't wanna be poor with no hope for the future. My best friend got pregnant at fourteen. She was smart too. And then she didn't wanna get an abortion because the boy said he loved her and would marry her. But he left anyway. Before the baby was born. Now she regrets not getting the abortion."

"You'll make it," he said absentmindedly.

"I'm just saying."

"I believe in you," he said.

"You don't even know me," she said.

"Yes, I do."

"I don't wanna go back to that shelter."

He got up and began clearing the table. "How do you get to school in Brooklyn from the Bronx?"

"I have to wake up at five a.m. to get started. It's horrible. I have to ride two buses and three trains to get to school."

"Why don't you change schools?"

"I like this school. I've been going there since junior high. From when we used to live on Snyder. I'm comfortable there. It's the only stable place I know. If I leave there I'll probably fall apart. Plus, there's this teacher. Mr. Jackson. My maths teacher. He's very nice to me. He's the only one I can talk to about my family situation. He encourages me. And pushes me to try hard. He tells me I have to work hard to get a good score on the SAT. He knows how bad I want to go to college. A few months ago, when I couldn't make it to class. . ."

"Why couldn't you make it to class? Were you sick?"

"Drama. Always drama. That's when we got kicked out of our apartment. We didn't have no place to go. Not even my grandmother would take us in. Said she didn't have no room for us. My mom went to stay with a friend, but she didn't have no room for me."

"And your mother stayed with this friend without you?"

"It was a male friend. I didn't like him. I didn't like the way he looked at me. Anyway, I don't blame her. She was trying to get back on her feet. Get a job. She desperately needed a place to stay."

"So did you."

'I told her I could stay with friends. Did that for a while. Shuttling between friends. Sometimes I'd ride the subway all night. Then I'd be in school the next day unable to keep my eyes open. Unable to concentrate."

"Damn!"

"So I decided to take some time off. I just couldn't make it. And Mr. Jackson, he would email me assignments and homework just to keep me going."

"How'd you get email if you didn't have a place to stay?"

"The library. Mr. Jackson would've taken me in if it wouldn't have looked bad. Him being a teacher and all."

"Did he..." Baseball paused. "He didn't, did he?"

"What?"

"You know. Try to..."

"Mr. Jackson? No. You crazy! He's not like that. He's really nice. There are some nice people in the world, you know." She laughed and twined her arms around his neck, kissing his nose. "Like you."

"Like me? How'm I nice? I made you blow me to stay in my apartment."

"You didn't make me."

He unwrapped her from around him and went to the bedroom. She trotted behind.

He pulled a backpack from the closet and began stuffing it with clothes. "Don't stay here too long. Might not be safe."

"I'm going wherever you're going," she declared.

He stopped. "That's crazy."

"Why's that crazy?"

"Because. . . It just is."

"I've never met anyone who's been as nice to me as you. You treat me special. You don't make me feel like I'm less than zero because I live in a shelter. We'll go somewhere together."

"Listen to yourself, Welcome. You don't know what you're talking."

"I know more than you think. I ain't no innocent little girl. I've seen things. I've seen a lot. Things that make me angry.

Things that make me cry. You see a lot of bad things when you live in a shelter. My fourteen-year-old brother is going to be a father. He got a thirty-something woman pregnant in the shelter. And he refuses to go to school. And my mother can't say nothing to him. I may only be sixteen but I've seen things."

"I thought you said you were seventeen."

"I'm sixteen going on fifty."

He laughed. "That's not good. I could go to jail for you."

"Who's telling?"

"You wanna go to college. You ain't gonna go to college if you stay around me, that's for damn sure."

"Why can't you tell me what you're running from? Are you running from the police?"

"I can't tell you, Welcome. But I'm not involved in drugs or anything like that. It's nothing like that."

"I can't force you to tell me," she said in resignation.

"It's for the best. I wish we could be together, Welcome. You don't know how much. But I gotta go somewhere to figure out my life. I can't tell you no more than that."

He finished filling his backpack in quiet. She watched him the entire time wiping tears from her eyes. She seemed so small and fragile now. He wanted to hold her, to hug her. To kiss her. But he dared not. He squeezed past her and went out into the hallway where he took his coat off the rack. She hadn't followed him.

Damn! The elevator was broken. He kept pressing the button though he knew the thing wasn't going to come. The sign pasted to the door said it should be fixed by 6 P.M.

To reach the stairs at one end of the hallway, he had to walk back past the apartment.

As he neared the apartment he heard singing. Was she singing? He put his ear to the door. She had a pretty good voice, too. He knocked on the door. It opened immediately. She stood there smiling.

"That you singing?"

"Yes."

"Why you singing?"

'cause I knew you'd come back."

"You knew I'd come back?"

"Yeah. I knew. I felt it in my heart."

"The elevator's broken," He said.

"I knew you'd come back."

"You broke the elevator?"

Her smile widened. "I got my things packed."

For a while he stood savoring her smile. "You ever been to Alaska?"